Illegal Tender

Gerald Hammond

Illegal Tender

MACMILLAN

First published 2000 by Macmillan
an imprint of Macmillan Publishers Ltd
25 Eccleston Place, London SW1W 9NF
Basingstoke and Oxford
Associated companies throughout the world
www.macmillan.co.uk

ISBN 0 333 90319 6

1 3 5 7 9 8 6 4 2

A CIP catalogue record for this book is available from
the British Library.

Typeset by Intype London Ltd
Printed and bound in Great Britain by
Mackays of Chatham plc, Chatham, Kent

Preface

Telling stories to the best of my limited ability is, comparatively speaking, a doddle, but mysteries are Hard Work – especially when one is well past the threescore and ten, at which time both concentration and short-term memory tend to fail.

So, unless I happen on another plot which writes itself (as happened with *The Reward Game* and several other books), this will be my last mystery story. It will be farewell to the Calder family, to the Cunninghams at Three Oaks Kennels and to Henry with whom I now have so much in common. I wish them well. Long may they continue flying the banner of Scottish fieldsports in the teeth of those who think that they know better.

When I set off on this path, more than twenty years ago, the term 'political correctness' had not yet been coined or at least had not yet come to my attention, but the dangerous concept was already in the air. I had to decide whether to pander to public misconceptions and show the shooting man as the stereotyped, rich idiot beloved of fiction and the media; but I never met anyone in that image and over the whole series I have tried to show the Scottish shooting and fishing fraternity (male and female) as I have come to know and love them – coming from all walks of life and more knowledgeable

1

and caring of wildlife than most of their critics. If I have done nothing to stem the tide I hope that I have at least left a record to contradict the propaganda of those who oppose a way of life which they have not experienced and can not comprehend.

While I was still wondering how to improve my meagre understanding of computer banking and its security, by coincidence a specialist in that field moved in next door. I am deeply grateful to Norman Edwardson for his help. Any remaining errors are mine alone.

I am also very grateful to a certain 'John Debri' who sent me the fraudulent e-mail reproduced with minor modifications in this book. Nice try, John!

Chapter One

'Uncle Henry?' said the voice on the phone.

I have never been blessed or cursed with nephews or nieces, so the voice had to belong to Elizabeth Ilwand (née Hay), granddaughter of one of my old and now deceased friends. 'Hello, Gooseberry,' I said.

I heard her laugh at the other end, a hundred miles away. The nickname is an old and private joke between us and one which seldom stales. 'Would you like to come through at the weekend?' she asked me. 'There are one or two bits of business.'

Elizabeth had been a sulky and rebellious girl, but the shock of her grandfather's death had begun a change which had come to fruition with her marriage the previous year. She was now a charming if imperious – not to say bossy – and sometimes headstrong young woman. Her grandfather had been an extremely wealthy man and she was his sole heir. In harness with the local solicitor, I had acted as his co-executor and was still one of her trustees. According to Sir Peter's will, those duties would not come to an end until two years after her marriage. That clause might not have stood up to scrutiny by a court, but Elizabeth seemed in no hurry to assume full responsibility for her inheritance. Our duties, however, had become progressively lighter as she had matured and come to understand the workings of an estate which comprised much of the Borders country for some miles around her home just outside the town of Newton Lauder. The signs were that she would become as caring a land-owner as her grandfather had been.

A quick, mental review of my engagements satisfied me that I had nothing inescapable imminent. On the other hand, it was late October, always a busy time at the Three Oaks Kennels where Isobel, my wife, is a partner; and although I have no formal position with the firm I am usually in demand for dog-walking, dummy-throwing, helping with the eternal feeding and cleansing and holding the fort when the partners and their helpers are otherwise engaged. This last activity usually peaks on Fridays and Saturdays.

'Would Monday do?' I asked her.

'If it suits you better. But we'll be holding the first shoot of the season on Saturday.'

I felt my interest stir like a spaniel at the sound of the gun-room door, but there were one or two points to be clarified. 'Syndicate? Or a let day?'

'The syndicate. And it looks as though several members will be away in France at the Rugby World Cup match. It's a driven day, so Mr Calder says that you wouldn't have to do much walking.'

That was certainly a consideration. Beaters are not always easily recruited and at weekends there is consider-able competition from other estates and from families in need of help with the shopping. Some shoots, especially early in the season before the birds become jumpy, may be wholly or partially walked-up and, although I can still manage a mile or two on pavement and rather more on grass, I am past the age for struggling through turnip-tops or spruce plantations. The Hay shoot at Newton Lauder, however, still commanded the loyalty of a squadron of beaters and both they and the syndicate members were always considerate to one who they regarded as having probably been a contemporary of Peter Hawker and having shot with Lord Ripon.

'I'll be through on Friday afternoon unless you hear to the contrary within the next hour,' I told her.

'That's fine,' she said. 'Usual drill.' Which meant 'No need to bring a dog or a dinner-jacket.'

As my friends are aware, my time for taking phone calls is after breakfast, when Isobel has left for the kennels and before I set off, as is my usual custom, to join her there. Elizabeth had caught me with my boots on and my stick in my hand, but I paused to phone Gordon Bream, to say that I would be passing through Edinburgh on the Friday and could make myself available for the discussion that he had been suggesting. Then, with something more to look forward to than the pleasant but humdrum demands of the dogs, I set off with what passes for a spring in my step.

There were no entries to competitions scheduled for the Saturday, John was not judging at any field trials and neither he nor Isobel were scheduled to go picking-up. No brood bitch was on the brink of whelping and the two kennel-maids would both be available for duty. My services, it seemed, could be dispensed with. I was relieved if mildly insulted.

Isobel was not going to let me go unburdened. She was inclined to remember the days when Sir Peter, and even more so 'Her La'ship', had entertained in some style in a draughty baronial mansion which had since burned down, to the great relief of most of those concerned. As a result, I took with me on the Friday morning two cases of 'good' clothes (as opposed to the old and comfortable garments that I intended to wear for most of the time and which fitted into a third and much smaller bag). My boots, as usual, went loose onto the floor behind the driver's seat.

It was a beautiful day. A summer of drizzle and fog had proved disastrous to the crops, but autumn was trying belatedly to make up for it, too late to save the farmers. Driving south into full sunshine becomes a penance when the sun gets lower in the sky, but I put on my Polaroids, pulled down the sun-visor and got through the Forth Bridge traffic and into Edinburgh in an hour. I had purposely arranged to meet Gordon at his office which was conveniently adjacent to a multi-storey car-park – my joints react unhappily to the impact of my feet on concrete.

I had rather hoped for an early adjournment in time for a drink before lunch but Gordon led me into his spacious and luxuriously furnished office. He was tall and thin with drooping moustache and yet a face that always looked ready to laugh. This contrasted with his way of life. As the most senior partner in a prestigious firm of accountants he had seats on several boards, was frequently appointed as an arbiter and was reputed to be financial adviser to God.

The discussion to follow would, I knew, amount to a board meeting of Agrotechnics (Farm Machinery) Ltd, because the other three board members (including Elizabeth) would never have dared to contradict Gordon and invariably went along with our lightest suggestions.

'We have to do something about Cowieson Farm Supplies,' Gordon said. 'In my opinion, the hour of doom has already passed. I've invited Maurice Cowieson to join us for a few minutes for some tough talking. Will you join me in taking a hard line?'

'Of course,' I said. 'You do the talking and I'll follow your lead.'

Agrotechnics had been founded by Sir Peter Hay to combat unemployment in his beloved area of the Borders by manufacturing the latest and best in agricultural equipment. His wishes were still respected. Rather than cause job losses in parallel industries, he had allowed considerable latitude to his debtors; a principle which we had followed reluctantly but faithfully. Unhappily, however, a local firm which had been retailing the agricultural machinery of Agrotechnics had been getting into serious difficulties.

Maurice Cowieson – Chairman, Managing Director and principal shareholder in Cowieson Farm Supplies Ltd – arrived a few minutes later. He was a tall man with a full head of white hair and, although he must have been in his fifties at least, the vitality of a man half his age. He had the reputation of one who lives life to the full or a little beyond and I could see the signs in the scarlet veins showing in his nose and eyeballs and in the beginning of a pot belly on a frame which was otherwise mostly skin and bone. His unlined face, however, which might well have resembled a skull, was fully fleshed and imprinted with an expression of affable charm.

At Gordon's invitation he lowered himself into one of the leather chairs and carefully straightened the creases in his trousers. 'Well now,' he said cheerfully. 'What's this meeting about? How can I help?' His cultivated charm was spoiled by a rasping voice.

'I think that you must have a very good idea what it's about,' Gordon said. Any suggestion of laughter had vanished from his face. 'Your outstanding account with Agrotechnics is now nearing the value of the firm and stock.'

'Oh that,' Cowieson said. 'I hope to settle all my accounts very shortly. There was a fire . . .' He left the sentence hanging in the air.

Gordon managed to keep exasperation out of his voice. 'I am well aware that there was a fire.'

'The fire doesn't account for more than a quarter of your debt,' I pointed out.

He ignored my inconvenient remark. 'When the insurance pays up . . .'

'Mr Cowieson,' Gordon said, 'you know as well as I do that your insurers are not going to pay up. They have made that clear. The fire in your warehouse was started by a disgruntled employee and arson was specifically excluded from your policy.'

Cowieson looked slightly less urbane. 'I shall be taking them to court.'

'That would be no more than throwing good money after bad as an expensive delaying tactic and we are not going to wait around for it. In any case, as Mr Kitts has said, the fire was only partially responsible for your troubles.'

The smile remained fixed on his lips but it had vanished from his eyes. 'What, may I ask, would you say was responsible for the remainder?'

'Plain bad management, of course,' Gordon said. 'You've been trying to run the firm with inadequate staff.'

Cowieson looked amused. 'In one breath you tell me that I have financial problems and in the next you tell me to take on more staff.'

'The time to take on more staff,' Gordon said patiently, 'would have been several years ago. If the few staff that you have hadn't been so overworked and unfulfilled because of being prevented from carrying out their functions effectively, one of them might not have been so disastrously disgruntled. That sort of penny-pinching only keeps overheads down and miscalculations up.'

Sensing that charm was no more than wasted effort, Cowieson resorted to being plaintive. 'My iniquitous contract with you requires me to take a certain minimum value of stock in every period of three months or lose the agency. Unsold stock accumulates.'

'It will,' I said, 'while you're not selling effectively. None of our agencies in other parts of Scotland has any difficulty meeting a similar quota.'

It was time to try injured dignity. Cowieson lifted his chin. 'I don't think that there's any point in prolonging this meeting. I'm already in discussion with the Swiss about getting fresh backing. I expect to have a favourable reply any day now.'

'For your sake,' Gordon said, 'I hope that's true. Shortly after the fire you granted a "floating charge". In case you didn't understand what your lawyers were putting before you, that means that you pledged the firm, inclusive of buildings and stock. If the debt is not reduced very substantially and soon, Agrotechnics will take over.'

If Cowieson was at all shaken by the threat, he showed no sign of it. 'There's no need for such a drastic step, gentlemen,' he said. 'Just have patience for a little longer and I'll pay my debts in full. And now, would you care to join me for lunch?'

'I'm afraid not,' Gordon said with great firmness. 'You really can't afford to buy business lunches any more and we're certainly not going to entertain Agrotechnics's debtors.'

For the first time, Cowieson looked put out. He pursed his lips and stood up. 'In that case, please excuse me. I have a living to earn.' He stalked out of the room.

'The cheek of the man!' Gordon said.

Gordon's favourite restaurant was only a step from his office. (Or possibly vice versa. It was suspected by his staff that the presence of the restaurant had been a major factor in choosing the location of the office.) Needless to say, it was excellent, providing mainly a French cuisine but incorporating the best from other nationalities.

'So he thinks that he can stall us off with talks about talks, with the Swiss or anybody else,' Gordon said. 'I don't see it coming to anything, myself. I suggest that we tell him to come up with the money within – what shall we say? – two weeks. Failing which, we'll crystallize the floating charge, take over and put our own managers in, which should ginger things up considerably.'

'I'll go along with that,' I said. 'Will you tell him or shall I? I'll be in his neighbourhood for the next few days.'

'I'll write to him formally,' Gordon said, 'and confirm it by fax. Which reminds me. Have you seen one of these?'

From his pocket he produced a folded length of computer paper. I opened it out and saw that it was a conventional e-mail. It was in Internet format, opening with an address followed by half a page of superfluous details giving incomprehensible information as to how the message had been encrypted and transmitted. My eye skipped to the body of the message. It read:

Dear CompuServe community member, our records show that billing information you have provided to us is not correct. This may be caused by one of the following reasons:

1. You haven't fill correctly our sign-up form.
2. By some error during connection, the information received was incorrect.
3. Your bank didn't reply correctly to our billing identification request.

Anyway, to continue using CompuServe you should fill the the following form. If you wish to cancel your account fill this table anyway and in the end write word CANCEL.

Member Identification
   User ID:
   Password:

Membership Information

   Country:
   First Name:
   Last Name:
   Address:
   City:
   State (USA Only):
   Zip or Postcode:

Evening Phone No:
Daytime Phone No:

Billing information

Name On Card:
Credit Card Type: (Gold, Platinum):
Card Number:
Expiration Date(MM/DD/YY):
Bank Name:
Account Number:
Sorting Code:
Password:
Social Security Number (USA Only):
Bank Phone No:

We are sorry for inconvenience and hope that you will continue to enjoy CompuServe.

Account Manager, John Debri

As the reader will have gathered, my wife is younger than I am. She comes almost from another generation, and I have learned from Isobel how to fumble my way around a computer, to use it as a super-typewriter and even to send an occasional e-mail, but that does not make me Internet-literate. Certain anomalies, however, were evident even to me. 'It doesn't ring true,' I said. 'For one thing, why would CompuServe – who, as I understand it, are what's known as a "service provider" – use an Internet format instead of their own? And why would they want both bank and credit card details? They would surely know how the account has been settled in the past. And it's barely literate – the writer's first language isn't English. Somebody's preparing a scam.'

Gordon nodded approvingly, even slightly patronizingly. 'You're absolutely right. It's an attempted fraud. It was sent to one of my partners. He phoned CompuServe and they said that it happens regularly. Sometimes people fall for it. If he sends out a hundred of these and only, say, two people give him the information he asks for, he can clean out their bank accounts or obtain some very expensive goodies on their credit card accounts. The police told George that they've traced some of the e-mails as originating from the Vancouver area, but that's very little help. If the culprit has a laptop computer, he could send them from any cybercafé, or a terminal in an airport, almost anywhere, gather up the returned information somewhere quite different and be long gone before anybody tries to catch up with him.'

We had reached the coffee stage but I was in no hurry to move. I was mildly intrigued. I had seen many attempts at fraud during my working days but life in the Fife countryside tended to insulate me from that sort of stimulus. The chairs were comfortable and a period of rest would be a substitute for my usual postprandial nap. One tires easily after threescore and ten. 'How would he have got your partner's e-mail address?'

'Not difficult. People often include them on their letterheads. And Internet correspondence in what they call the forums is open to any reader. But anyone with the skill to juggle the money electronically would surely be able to hack into more personal e-mail correspondence.'

Telephone banking had only been making an early appearance when I retired. It still required a mental effort to appreciate the huge sums which are now transmitted

– indeed, which only exist – in the form of electronic signals. 'I thought that the really clued-up fraudster hacked straight into the computer of a bank, insurance company or building society and transferred money direct from account to account,' I said.

Gordon nodded. As an accountant who was still among the world's workers, he was more up to date than I was. 'That's a much more sophisticated operation,' he said, 'quite beyond most amateurs.' He tapped the paper. 'Any fool could carry out this one.'

'This fool certainly couldn't,' I told him. 'May I keep this?'

'Surely. I have other copies. I only carry it around so that I can warn people not to be caught out.'

'That's what I want it for,' I said.

I turned off the main road, which was heading in the direction of Newcastle, threaded my way through the old Borders town of Newton Lauder and climbed a hill beyond the outskirts.

A monumental archway, looking pompous and out of place, marked the end of the drive to Hay Lodge. (The original edifice, now gone, had been known as Hay Castle but, when he caused the new house to be constructed on the site, Peter had bowed to Lady Hay's insistence that the name Hay be retained but had jibbed at the alliteration of Hay House or Hay Hall.) As I slowed to turn through the archway a red Mini shot out and across my bows, driven by a young woman with a determined expression and a cigarette in her mouth. I heard her make racing changes up the gears as she vanished towards the town. I made more stately progress towards the house.

I still half expected Hay Castle, the old monstrosity, complete with turrets and crow-stepped gables, to be standing at the end of the driveway. (Peter had referred to it as The Hay Stack, but never when Her La'ship was within earshot.) The sweep of bright blue sky was definitely an improvement as was the comfortable modern house set to one side of the sweep of gravel. The new house, of stone and glass and silver-weathered cedar, looked, as always, as though it had been placed there first and the countryside arranged around it later. I could not pay any architect a higher compliment than that.

The footings of the Victorian pile, which had burned down some years earlier regretted by none save only Her La'ship (who, as I recalled, had been the most almighty snob), had been incorporated into a flower garden which, despite the advanced state of the year, still showed some roses. Most of the garden's colour depended on the berries in beds of massed cotoneasters and berberis but a small stand of maples had been planted behind the house and these were in full flame. The birches, always the first to fall, were bare but the wood facing the lawn behind the house was green and gold.

The former Elizabeth Hay, now Mrs Ilwand, had been an attractive girl. She would have been more so but for a very determined chin. Aided by Ralph Enterkin (my fellow trustee), I had steered her away from an unfortunate liaison with an obvious fortune-hunter and towards her new husband; but the steering had required a very delicate touch. The result had so far proved successful. Duncan Ilwand was a very good-looking young man, possibly too good-looking for his own good although, to do him justice, he seemed quite unaware of his good fortune. He had no money of his own but he was well connected and so had a proper respect for property. He and Elizabeth had been fellow students.

It was a recurrent shock not to see Peter Hay's scarecrow figure standing in his well-worn kilt at the front door, but Elizabeth must have been awaiting my arrival. She met me at the door. I was reminded again of the contradictions in her character when she insisted that I go for the rest which she knew I would be needing but was firmly insistent on my taking it when and where she directed and whether I wanted it or not. (There was more than a trace in her of her formidable grandmother, Her La'ship.) I can be quite as stubborn as she can, as she knew perfectly well because I had fended off the unsuitable suitor who had found favour with her; but on this occasion I was happy to have Ronnie, her factotum, carry my luggage up to my usual room and there to remove my shoes and settle on top of the bed for an hour of blissful oblivion broken only by what I took to be the sound of the returning Mini.

After precisely one hour, which Elizabeth considered to be the correct duration for an afternoon nap, Ronnie came knocking apologetically at my door with a message that Madam expected me for afternoon tea downstairs in fifteen minutes. Ronnie was a large man. He was no beauty. To describe him as rough-hewn was almost flattery and he had a reputation as a formidable pub-fighter when in his cups, but he had a heart of purest gold. He had been Sir Peter's stalker and ghillie, but a life spent largely on the hill or up to his immense backside in cold water had not been kind to him and, as rheumatism and arthritis began to limit his usefulness outdoors on an estate in which his functions were diminishing, he had been more or less converted into gardener, assistant keeper and general dogsbody. He even functioned as butler on those occasions when buttling was required, and managed very well.

In accordance with some custom of his own, Ronnie brought with him a silver tray on which were two glasses of a very good malt whisky. I invited him to take a seat while I washed and made myself tidy. It had been some months since I last visited the house. Elizabeth would no doubt bring me up to date on the superficial gossip but, though he could keep his mouth shut when it mattered, I could count on Ronnie to tell me what was really going on. He knew that I had her interests very much at heart.

He needed little or no persuasion. 'Mr Ilwand and the Mistress are still lovey-dovey,' he said. 'You'd jalouse they was still on their honeymoon. She aye wants tae ken where he is, ilka minute o the day. It's no that she disna trust him, it's just her way. And we've a new house-keeper.'

He sounded disgruntled and I could understand why. The estate was largely a family affair, so much so that at one time I had considered marrying Elizabeth off to the surveyor who was acting as factor. Ronnie's wife Mary had been cook-housekeeper for some years, assisted by Joanna who was now married to Hamish, the game-keeper. Joanna, I happened to know, was Ronnie's daughter, born on the wrong side of the blanket. I sus-pected that the lady who came in daily to help with the domestic chores was somebody's cousin. It was all very cosy and almost incestuous.

'But Mary's still here?' I asked.

'Oh aye. But noo she's jist the cook.'

'Is that so bad? She and Joanna can take it a bit easier now.'

'No a bit of it,' Ronnie said. 'The new wumman – Miss Payne she's called and a pain she is – doesna fash hersel wi work or oniething like it, just handing out orders to Mary and Joanna. She was a collegianer – a student, ye ken? – in digs wi the Mistress but she failed the course or got herself expelled, something the like o that, an the Mistress met her again at some do in Edinburgh, found she was oot o work an fetched her here. Ye'll mak her acquaintance soon enough. She dines wi the family an sits aboot the rest o the day, smoking like a lum. Or oot she gangs in her wee car, driving like a bampot an wearing a Barbour coat jist like the queen's an nivver walks a yard if she can ride.' He glanced at his very expensive wristwatch, a legacy from his late employer, and finished his drink at a single gulp. 'Ye'll need to be moving or ye'll get your erse skelped.'

I took the hint and made my way downstairs.

Elizabeth was already seated in the sunny sitting room, where the big windows showed a view over the flower garden, down the valley and over the town of Newton Lauder to the hills beyond. It was a view which I had always envied. We have a view across the fields from our home in Fife, but nothing like that.

There was tea on the low table and thin sandwiches. Dispensing both from one of the comfortable wing-chairs was a woman in her early twenties, small and neat-boned. She had blonde hair in a frizzled perm. Under an expression of discontent I discerned features which were feminine, delicate and somehow piquant. In younger days I would have described her mouth as kissable. I thought that her figure might turn out to be rather better than merely good, once one looked deeper than the long denim skirt and the denim jacket over a polo-neck sweater. Her floral perfume struggled with and overcame the smoke from her cigarette. Here, I decided, was a potentially attractive woman who either failed to make the most of her charms or else played them down, perhaps so as not to compete with her hostess or perhaps out of a contempt for men, although this seemed unlikely. Out of long though not recent experience I thought that I recognized something in her poise and expression which I had never seen except in one or two women whose passion was deeply buried but waiting to explode. When Elizabeth introduced her as Beatrice Payne, she offered me a slender hand to shake or possibly to kiss, I couldn't be sure which. I received a friendlier greeting from the two dogs. Nick, the older Labrador, I knew had been granted the mercy of euthanasia during the previous month, but the other Labrador and the spaniel were old friends and in good health. Spin, the spaniel, when he had given me a courteous sniff, a butt of the head and a few thumps of the tail, went back to lie beside Miss Payne with his chin resting on her foot. She seemed unaware of the contact.

Miss Payne seemed to have made herself at home – excessively so, I thought, for a housekeeper. Cigarettes and a box of matches were neatly aligned with the edge of the table beside her hand together with an ashtray half full of stubs and broken, burned matches. Her manner suggested that she was part-hostess rather than an employee, but I supposed that as a former fellow-student on hard times her position was more of a sinecure, disguising the fact that she was down on her luck and therefore, effectively, a sponger. That alone, I thought charitably, would be enough to make her defensive.

Elizabeth's phone call had suggested that there were a number of items of estate business to be cleared between us and I had several of my own to mention, but I had no intention of discussing business in the presence of Miss Payne and I could hardly suggest that she leave us. Thus the conversation was limited to the usual stilted topics – the weather, the harvest just past, traffic in the town, health and the likelihood of another flu epidemic in the coming winter.

I would have to catch Elizabeth on her own and solicit a private discussion. Meantime, rather than continue a tea party which I found heavy going, I suggested that I take the dogs for a walk.

Elizabeth nodded benignly. 'We'll be dining at about seven,' she said. 'Just the four of us, so don't change. Tomorrow, we'll be having the usual dinner after the shoot for those who want to stay on – mostly those who don't have to drive.'

'Does Mr Kitts stay for the dinner?' Miss Payne enquired. She lit another cigarette, snapped the match and dropped it into the ashtray. Her tone made it clear that she could bear my absence with equanimity.

Her tone put my back straight up. I was on the point of remarking that I would stay at least until I had had a chance of airing with her employer, in privacy, the matters that I had been invited through to discuss, but Elizabeth beat me to it. 'Uncle Henry is welcome to stay for as long as he likes, any time,' she said sharply. 'Can you stay over, at least until Monday or Tuesday?' she asked me. 'I have several things to talk over but the urgency has rather gone out of them. The cheque for

Talisman Farm hadn't arrived but it came through the day after I phoned you.'

She had no need to say more. Talisman Farm is remote from the estate and Peter had only acquired it to save an old friend from financial embarrassment. Its management at such long range had always proved time consuming and cumbersome, so it had been agreed to accept a very favourable offer, earmarking the money for investment in Agrotechnics for building and equipping a major extension. But the sale of the farm had entailed selling-on a large part to the local authority and the resale of the remainder to a financial institution and subsequent leasing back. The four corners of the deal should have been complete at Michaelmas and the Agrotechnics extension was already rising above the ground. Delayed payments to the building contractor would have proved more expensive than the raising of short-term finance.

I said that I could stay for as long as it took. 'Who'll be on the shoot?' I asked.

Elizabeth reeled off names. Some I knew. Others, because there had been some changes among the syndicate members, were strange to me. And there were names that seemed familiar and yet I could not put faces to them. Recall becomes less certain with the passing years. Then she mentioned a name that made me sit up.

Cowieson. Miss Payne's hand paused in the act of raising her cigarette. Then she busied her hands rearranging and tidying the table. I thought that the name probably held significance for her also.

'Not Maurice Cowieson, of Cowieson Farm Supplies?' I asked.

Elizabeth shook her head. 'The son,' she said. 'Miles.'

'Is he in the business?'

'I think he's the sales manager.' She saw my face and asked, 'What's wrong?' I glanced at Miss Payne. 'It's all right,' Elizabeth said impatiently. 'Bea's very discreet.'

In my experience, it's very rare for someone to be as discreet as the impression they manage to convey, but I had no option. 'Unless the older man pulls off a miracle very quickly, the firm's in for trouble. They're heavily in debt to Agrotechnics and you'll remember that they granted a floating charge, virtually putting up the firm itself as security. It was all spelled out at the July board meeting. Now, by Gordon Bream's reckoning – and he's usually right to within a fiver on these sorts of things – the debt's approaching the value of the business. They're being warned that unless they come up with the money in two weeks the board will be asked to call up the floating charge.'

'In other words, to foreclose?'

'Near enough. You're on the board of Agrotechnics. I was waiting for a chance to get your view.'

She frowned. 'I'd want to be assured that the existing staff wouldn't suffer,' she said. 'We can discuss it on Sunday. Life's going to be rather hectic until then. To go back to what started us off about it, Miles Cowieson's a syndicate member. He took over Jeremy Graeme's gun when the old chap had to give up. And I've already asked him to the dinner so I can't uninvite him. Don't worry about it. He probably won't know who you are.'

'His father certainly knows,' I said. 'I hate getting embroiled in a business argument on a social occasion. I want to relax and enjoy myself without having to keep my guard up. You'll be doing me a favour if you try to keep him away from me and make sure that he's at the other end of the dinner table.'

Instead of instructing the supposed housekeeper, Elizabeth promised to try.

Miss Payne had hardly said a word and it seemed only polite to draw her into the conversation. 'Will you be out with the Guns tomorrow?' I asked her.

She shook her head. 'I don't hold with reared game-shooting.'

I was intrigued. Most people, if they object to shooting, object to the whole scene. 'But not rough-shooting?' I asked.

'I was brought up on a farm,' she said calmly. 'How could I object to one or two men going out to see what wild meat they can collect? But game-rearing lowers the whole thing to the level of poultry farming.'

'The pheasant isn't a very good mother,' I pointed out. 'And, with the gamekeeping profession reduced to a shadow of its old self, ground-nesting game-birds and their broods are at the mercy of every fox, stoat, weasel, feral cat, sparrowhawk or buzzard to come looking for an easy meal.' I paused. I seemed to have forgotten half a dozen other predators but my mind had gone blank on the subject. 'I take your point but I can't see any real objection to taking some of the hen pheasants into a protected environment for a few months and then releasing them and their poults back into the wild.'

'No,' she said coldly. 'I don't suppose you can.' She rose to her feet and left the room, taking with her the almost overflowing ashtray and an apple from the bowl.

I raised my eyebrows at Elizabeth. 'Not a very friendly young woman,' I suggested.

Elizabeth smiled faintly. 'Don't think too badly of her,' she said. 'Bea never did talk much and just at the moment – I may as well tell you in case you say the wrong thing –

she's expecting a baby. There's a boyfriend somewhere but I sense trouble. She won't talk about it.'

I made my escape rather than ask whether Elizabeth thought that the boyfriend might also be the father.

I put my head into the kitchen to say hello to Mary and Joanna and then went out into the cool autumn sunshine. The dogs were old friends – indeed Spin, the spaniel, had been bred at Three Oaks and I had had a hand in his training. Looking back, I rather thought that I had been present at his birth. He had been the cherished acquisition of Sir Peter Hay and, almost immediately thereafter, a legacy to Hamish, Joanna's husband and Elizabeth's gamekeeper. The Labrador, Royston, had been passed on to Ronnie, but both dogs, while their owners were at work and if not themselves required in the field or being walked by anyone setting off in a suitable direction, spent their days in their former home. They gambolled round me (Royston in a stiff and elderly manner resembling my own dignified pace, but Spin more like the puppy which he had been not long ago) before settling down to the serious business of exploring all the scents in the wood behind the house and the hedgerows leading from it, to find out what had changed since their last walk a few hours earlier.

I turned away from the place where Peter Hay had died. I had never willingly returned to where I had found the body of my old friend. My way brought me down to Hamish's cottage (now shared by Joanna). The brooder houses would be empty now, the pheasants loose in the woods and farmland since early July, but Hamish and Ronnie were busily loading sacks of grain into the back of Hamish's long-chassis Land Rover pickup. The feed hoppers would have to be topped up and it was Hamish's habit, when the birds had gone up to roost on the evening before a shoot, to lay trails of grain which in the morning would encourage them out of their coverts and out to where he wanted to begin his drives. No bird, he contended, flew as well as one which was going home.

Hamish, I was amused to note, had been allowed to regrow the beard which he had shaved off during his courtship of Joanna.

We exchanged a few words about the prospects for the next day. The light faded while the few words grew into an animated discussion of the estate's planting policy. I was not considered hale enough to lift sacks of grain but I could still carry a bucket, so I went the rounds with them under a shining moon and only got back to the house in time to wash and let Joanna brush the chaff off my tweeds. Joanna, lush of body and with luminous eyes in a face which departed just enough from beauty to be interesting, had been a dangerous sexpot but I was relieved to see, now she was a respectable married lady, that her manner was less flirtatious and she was almost prudishly careful where she stroked with the brush.

Duncan, Elizabeth's husband of less than a year, had returned from work. After he graduated in Electronics and Computing and the pair were married, none of the usual careers open to him (most of which might have taken them anywhere in the world) seemed appropriate. He could have settled down and taken a hand in the running of the estate but, as he told me when I had a fatherly chat with him before the wedding, to have a wife who was also his employer would put an unfair strain on both of them. Instead, he had taken a partnership with Jake Paterson, who was beginning to think seriously of retiring. Jake operated the TV and radio shop in Newton Lauder, installed and maintained security systems and did most of the computer sales and maintenance for miles around. Elizabeth had provided the money for the partnership agreement but I was pleased and relieved to learn that, thereafter, Duncan had refused to accept more than his keep and the occasional unsolicited gift from her.

Duncan gave me an unaccustomed grin of welcome and I saw for the first time why he so rarely opened his lips when he smiled. White but uneven teeth were the only flaw in a face of almost film-star handsomeness.

Miss Payne handed round the drinks. When we moved through to the dining room she came with us and settled at one of the four places set, leaving Joanna to serve the meal. There was an excellent wine. Either Peter Hay's cellar or his standards were surviving.

At first, the dinner-table conversation was no more than a catching-up with minor news. We were enjoying a cordon bleu trout with almonds when Duncan said, 'Hugh McPhail, from Potter's Farm, was in the shop today. The computer he uses for farm records and accounts has crashed. He thinks somebody sent him a virus.'

'Maybe they did,' Elizabeth said.

Duncan shook his head. 'He hadn't been doing more than receiving and opening e-mail. You don't admit a virus without running a macro infected with a malicious code.'

'Didn't he keep backup disks?' Elizabeth asked.

'Some. But he's not sure if they're complete or not.

He wants to know, can we let him have copies of any accounts over the last year or so?'

'I could let him have some of them. But he'd be better approaching Jim Frazier at the factor's office.'

'I'll tell him,' Duncan said. 'He took up about an hour – which I could have put to better use – telling me what a hard time farmers are having.'

'I'm sorry for the farmers,' Elizabeth said. 'It's a terrible time. Perhaps it's time that we reviewed some of the farm rentals.'

It was unusual for her to take the soft-hearted view but I had some sympathy with that viewpoint. Farmers, after years of easy prosperity, were now faced by a world in which one food crisis after another had forced meat prices down. Many fields had been turned over to cereal crops only to meet with a succession of poor harvest years. Farmers were being urged to diversify, but among so many there was only so much diversification to go around. The more far-seeing realized that future profit depended on efficiency. The result was that, despite a general shortage of money, many were re-equipping and Agrotechnics was busy. It was a climate in which only a man like Maurice Cowieson could deal in agricultural machinery and not make money.

On the other hand, while compassion can be a virtue in a landowner it is not always to be recommended as a business principle. Peter Hay had somehow managed to steer a course which avoided the worst pitfalls – to mix my metaphors. 'Farmers are congenital grumblers,' I said, 'and Hugh McPhail's the worst of the lot. Any farmer will tell you he's heading for Queer Street while leaning against the back of his Ferrari. And you daren't suggest for a moment that they brought the BSE crisis on themselves and lost their markets due to bad feeding practices. You could consider allowing some credit at a reduced rate of interest.'

Elizabeth looked at me sharply. I was happy to see that she was developing some of her grandfather's sense of paternalism, provided only that she did not let it run away with her. 'And when one of them can't keep up? What then? Slam the door, as with Cowieson's?'

'If necessary.'

'What would my grandfather have done?'

Without intending it, she had let me off the hook. 'He would have looked damned hard at each of them,' I said. 'Those who were working hard and acting wisely but still in difficulties through bad luck, he would have treated with sympathy. The fools, the extravagant or the lazy he would have been happy to get rid of and replace with somebody more efficient. Before going that far,' I added awkwardly – I had no desire to be regarded as Shylock's big brother – 'you could first think about hiring somebody from one of the agricultural colleges to go round and recommend improvements to farm policies and working practices. In the long run, that might be a sound investment. If they reject his advice it might be time enough for something more drastic.'

'That's more like it,' Elizabeth said with satisfaction. 'I always knew that you had a heart buried somewhere.'

I thanked her, without bothering to mention that in the present that economic climate the re-letting of farms might not attract the same rentals as in more affluent times. I have always been quite happy to take credit when it is not my due.

Miss Payne caught me by surprise by muttering an apology and hurrying out of the room. 'Poor Bea,' Elizabeth said. 'Her father used to farm near here. He was caught out by the BSE calamity. He had a lot of land but it was stony ground, not suitable for anything but pasture. He went to the wall, of course. I think it was the shame of it that finished Bea at university.'

That might explain the discontented expression, but any young woman of energy and resource should be able to put any such disaster behind her and get on with making a life for herself. I wondered whether Elizabeth was really doing her a favour by sheltering her from the need to earn a proper living. Then I remembered the expected little bundle of joy and felt ashamed of the thought. Single parenthood did not carry the same stigma as in my young day. Some girls might embrace it deliberately. But to most it signified an appalling hurdle in the way of dreams.

Chapter Two

Saturday morning came in crisp and bright with just the sort of breeze a keeper prays for to help the birds fly well. At breakfast – served by Joanna who was still unaided by the ostensible housekeeper – the usual air of suppressed excitement seemed to pervade the house. Since the dawn of mankind, the hunt and the feast which succeeded it were the peaks which rose above the ground of mere survival. No matter that the so-called civilizing process has diminished driven game-shooting to a formalized compromise between the pursuit of meat and poultry farming, it remains a sociable, satisfying and highly demanding activity.

Hamish and Ronnie, I knew, would have been out since dawn, dogging-in the boundaries. Thirty years earlier, twenty even, I would have been with them.

By long-standing arrangement I had not brought a gun but borrowed my late friend's Churchill, a top quality gun which happened both to fit and to suit me very well. In deference to her grandfather's expressed wish that things continue much as during his lifetime, Elizabeth had obtained the necessary certificates and retained his guns, but she had never learned to use them – unlike her husband, who was an excellent shot and very much at home in his capacity as host.

The day went well. The bag was comparatively small. Many of the members were seriously out of practice after the long spring and summer layoff. (Hamish, I knew would be pleased. A bird missed today will be there to swell the numbers later in the season.) Nevertheless, the atmosphere among Guns and beaters was almost festive and the buffet lunch in the big barn was a jolly occasion. In the shooting field a person is judged more by their proficiency and obedience to the unwritten rules than by such criteria as money or social status. I was amused to see one of the beaters being served his meal by one of the Guns, but I knew that the beater was a neighbouring landowner whose intractable master-eye problem and absolute refusal to use a crossover stock would not have prevented him from shooting but would have made certain that he never hit anything, while his butler, who had received a substantial legacy from a previous employer but stayed in post because he knew no other life, was a paid-up member of the syndicate. Neither seemed to think the arrangement unusual.

But perhaps I remember the day as being one of the best because of my own triumph. On the last drive, Hamish placed me at a gap in a hedgerow, in full view of Guns and beaters alike, to act as a stop and deter the pheasants from legging it downhill and away from the covert. Instead of trying to escape on foot, a good proportion of birds decided to take wing along the line of the hedge. Because the ground was falling, they came over high.

For once, I found myself on form and the cartridges came to hand the right way round and found the chambers of the Churchill of their own accord. The light, short-barrelled gun seemed to point itself. The sun, for once, was at my back. I had no animus against the birds, only respect. This was their destiny and without this end they would never have known existence. When the final whistle blew there were eleven birds stone dead on the grass and eleven spent cases at my feet. Elizabeth, who was giving the old Labrador an easy day at the picking-up, gathered them and I helped her to carry them to the game-cart. I rejoined the throng at the cars to receive a round of applause – a rare tribute and even rarer and more precious for one who had thought that his years of creditable shooting were behind him. Life had little more to offer.

At the close of the driven day, Hamish took some of the younger and keener guns off to waylay the ducks coming in to feed on a nearby loch. Two syndicate members went home to change and return to dinner. Along with another guest who was staying overnight, I went back to the house for a bath, a rest and a change of clothes, reliving meanwhile every moment of that last drive. For the moment, I was a happy man.

I had plenty of time for a nap.

Bearing in mind that about half the male dinner guests would have had no chance to change out of shooting clothes, I had brought a carefully chosen suit – clean and presentable but far from dapper. Thus clad, I came downstairs and looked into the dining room. The table was extended to its fullest and sixteen places were laid. Ronnie, who had helped to control the beating line all day, was now hastily scrubbed and dressed in his butler suit and was putting the finishing touches to the settings.

'Do you want a hand with cleaning all the guns?' I asked him.

Ronnie looked shocked that a guest should suggest such a thing. 'I'll manage.' He shooed me though to the big sitting room where the party was assembling.

During my many years in banking, I had noticed that one of the dangers in being seriously rich is that most of their number have difficulty in deciding just how rich they are and either blow the lot in an orgy of extravagance or resort to a quite unnecessary counting of the pennies. I was relieved to note that Elizabeth and Duncan were keeping a sense of proportion. There must have been a temptation to be ostentatious and serve champagne, turning the syndicate shoot, which returned a modest profit to the estate, into a financial millstone, but I was content to accept a middle-of-the-road, sparkling Italian wine as a substitute although I suspected that it would quickly provoke an acid stomach.

I was nursing my glass, spinning it out until dinner should be announced, when a man in his early thirties pushed through the throng, squeezed between two rather stout wives and planted himself in front of me. 'It's Mr Kitts, isn't it?' he said.

I had watched him identifying me from across the room, so there would be no point denying it. I had tried to hide behind a large and very articulate lady who was lecturing me on the economics of comparison shopping and whom I had seen driving a most unsuitable XJS which I would have given my eye teeth to own, but to no avail. He bore a strong resemblance to his father. He was as tall and almost as thin and, because he was very fair, his mop of hair was reminiscent of his father's, but he lacked the broken veins and the small pot belly. I let him introduce himself. 'I'm Miles Cowieson,' he said.

'I . . . I saw you at work during the last drive. That was quite a display of shooting.'

'I don't always shoot like that,' I said, modestly but with perfect truth.

'I never knew anyone who did.' He stirred uneasily and his face flushed. 'I believe that you're a director of Agrotechnics?'

Now that he had changed the subject, I was less willing to give him my attention. 'I don't think that this is exactly the time or place—' I began.

He broke in hastily. 'Just let me plant one little thought and then I'll leave you in peace. If the debt is going to be called in and Agrotechnics is going to take over my father's firm—'

It was my turn to break in. 'That would be a board decision, not up to me.'

'I know that. Please listen. It could be the best thing since I-don't-know-what.' He must have seen my surprise, for he smiled. His smile had the charm of his father's but in his case it was quite unconscious and uncultivated. 'I mean it,' he said. 'Dad's a fine man but he's a stick-in-the-mud. I've had a thousand ideas for promoting sales – competitions, advertising with a real kick to it, junk e-mail, you name it – but he turns them all down. When we get a farmer half sold, I'd like to demonstrate the machinery on his farm and invite all the neighbouring farmers to come and watch, with lunch to follow. Dad won't hear of it. If you take the firm over, you could keep me on as Sales Manager and I'll show you how selling should be done.' There was an envelope in his hand. 'Take this. It's my action plan. Read it at your leisure. I've set out a dozen ideas for putting the firm back on its feet but the old man won't look at any of them. He still expects the world to beat a path to his door. At least let me give them a try.'

'It still wouldn't be my decision,' I said. 'Anyway, aren't you being a bit premature? Your father may still raise the finance he's looking for.'

'Well, I for one am not holding my breath. I don't know where he thinks it's coming from.'

'The Swiss, he said.'

Miles looked doubtful. 'I don't see Swiss money being interested. The Japanese, perhaps. It might be better not to enquire. Anyway, it would only saddle the firm with more debt. Thanks for listening to me.'

'You may get your chance,' I said. 'Are you a partner or salaried staff?'

'I'm on a salary. Dad was always promising but so far he's refused to make me a partner.'

'That may turn out to be for the best,' I told him. 'If we do take over – and it's a big if – at least one other board member is determined that no staff lose their jobs. Provided that they're competent staff, I go along with that.'

He thought it over and suddenly smiled. 'You mean that if the takeover goes ahead, he'd be out and I'd be in?'

'If,' I said.

His smile broadened. 'Well, many thanks. I'm going away for a few days of overdue holiday but I wanted to register my interest in case it all comes to a head while I'm away. Perhaps we can speak again when I come back.'

He melted back into the throng of men in informal dress and women who had somehow managed, even the two who had shot and those who had accompanied the Guns, to be modish and modestly jewelled. I saw him head for the drinks table and a moment later he was in cheerful conversation with Bea Payne who seemed also to be brightening. Miles left me with food for thought. According to his son, Mr Cowieson Senior might be looking for finance from the Japanese; but the Japanese are not moneylenders *per se*. If they propped up Cowieson's business, it would be as a first step towards gaining a stranglehold on the Agrotechnics share of the market in farm equipment – a useful diversification for a vehicle plant many miles away which was suffering a fall in orders, but a potential disaster locally. The ultimate result could turn out to be a wholesale transfer of work elsewhere and a return of unemployment to the area. I would have to speak with Gordon Bream, and soon, but off the top of my head I could see no way that we could impose conditions on how Maurice Cowieson raised the money to pay off his debt.

I had been right about the wine. I made a quick trip upstairs for some Gaviscon to soothe my acid stomach so that I missed Ronnie's announcement of dinner but I joined the drift into the dining room. I found that I was placed on my hostess's right with Keith Calder opposite and his daughter beside me. Keith was the shoot captain and I had come to know him well over the previous few years. Elizabeth had been as good as her word and Miles Cowieson was four places to my right.

It seemed that my moment of glory was not quite over. Keith looked across the table. 'We can't afford to have you as a guest if you're going to shoot like that,' he said. 'We want the birds to last until January.'

'Until the last drive,' I said, 'only one bird came near me and I missed it.'

'In that case we'll forgive you.' He smiled and turned

to the lady on his left. I fell into small talk with Elizabeth, but I could still feel a small glow lingering from Keith's approval. He and his family are counted as the finest shots for miles around.

Mary and Joanna, no doubt aided by some local help, had done us proud. The meal was excellent and the wines were passable, again without being extravagant. Ronnie, by keeping his mouth firmly shut, passed muster as a rather rough-hewn butler. If I half-closed my eyes I could almost believe that the grand old days of Her La'ship had returned.

We arrived at coffee in a murmur of good-natured conversation and an occasional spatter of laughter. I was speaking to Keith's daughter, Deborah. She had been one of the only two woman Guns that day. 'Ian wasn't out today,' I remarked.

'He had to go to a conference on electronic fraud,' she said. 'Mum and I tossed a coin for who went on the shoot and stayed for the dinner and who stayed at home to look after Bruce.'

'And you won?'

'She thinks that she won. She adores her grandson. Ian was fizzing. He'd been looking forward to today.' Her husband was a detective inspector, the only senior CID officer in Newton Lauder. When the pair had met, Deborah had told me, Ian had been tainted with the policeman's eternal view of firearms as tools of the devil, to be kept at all costs out of all hands except those of the police. But nobody could mingle with the Calders for long without the family's enthusiasm and philosophy rubbing off on them and Ian had become an enthusiastic and averagely competent performer at both game and clays.

The mention of his conference reminded me. I took

Gordon's pages of computer paper out of my pocket. 'This might interest you,' I said, addressing my immediate neighbours at the table. My words happened to fall into a gap in the general chatter and an expectant silence came down. Well, so be it. 'Who uses e-mail?' I asked the world in general.

From the nods and murmurs I gathered that most of the men present and about half the ladies were e-mail users.

'This is a deliberate attempt to set up a fraud,' I said. 'So it may pay you to be on your guard. Has anybody here had one of these?' Omitting the opening half-page of computer-babble, I read out the message, drawing a little humour out of the grammatical errors.

'I had one of those,' said a retired doctor and syndicate member at the opposite corner of the table. 'I used the reply facility to send back a message saying "Nice try!" and passed a copy to the police. Your husband, Mrs Fellowes, said that there had been many such attempts, targeting people all over the English-speaking world. Some of them have been successful. You'd wonder at people being so trusting. One of my neighbours, Mackillop, lost a couple of hundred – he's becoming known locally as Mac the Naif. DI Fellowes told me that the Met was co-ordinating the British end of the investigation. Apparently they traced the original message to somewhere in Canada.'

'Vancouver, I'm told,' I said.

'I believe that's right.'

Conversation had become general again, with several of the company reciting examples of who had had such e-mails, who knew somebody who had had one and a few who felt insulted at not having been considered worthy of the attempt. There was some competition at devising the most humorous and insulting replies.

Laughing at a contribution from Keith, I glanced at Elizabeth. She had gone so white that her make-up showed up as patches of unnatural colour. She looked as though she might faint. 'Are you all right?' I whispered.

She shook her head.

'Let me take you outside.'

'I can't leave the guests.'

'Of course you can.' I stood up. Conversation died. 'Mrs Ilwand is feeling faint,' I said. 'I'm taking her outside for a breath of air.'

Duncan began to get up but Elizabeth made a negative gesture. 'You stay,' she said. 'Don't break up the party on my account.'

I helped her to her feet. Most of the men half-rose politely. She leaned on my arm and I led her out of the room.

The room which had been Peter Hay's study and which now, virtually unchanged, acted as an office, was handy. I also suspected that we might need its facilities. I was going to settle her on the couch but she moved to the swivel chair behind the desk, lowered herself into it and put her head down for a moment on her knees. When she raised her head again, her hair was flying but she did not care. Her colour had made a partial return.

She licked her lips. 'You can guess?' she asked me.

'You've been had?'

'Almost certainly.' She snatched up the phone, keyed in a number and went through procedures which I recognized as being those for a telephone banking system. She listened and when she disconnected she was looking twenty years older. 'The account's been cleaned out,' she said. Suddenly she banged her fist on the desk. 'How could I have been so stupid?' she demanded of the room. In a way, I was relieved. The old crushproof Elizabeth was still capable of making a comeback.

'Surely it can't have been much of a loss,' I suggested. 'The estate can stand it. Tell the police and then write it off to experience.'

'You don't understand,' she said. 'I spoke to you – when was it? – on Tuesday. The cheque for Talisman Farm arrived, special delivery, the next morning. I took it to the bank and paid it straight into the estate account. A million and a quarter, near enough. I was waiting to ask you what to do about it so that it wouldn't be entirely idle until it was needed for the Agrotechnics flotation. That's what's gone.'

I felt a hollowness in my bowels and almost unbearable tension in my neck, both, I could tell, stemming from a sense of guilt. I was, after all, half of her trustees. But Elizabeth's returning anger was directed against herself, on top of which she was in a state of shock. When I touched her hand it was ice cold and trembling. If I gave way to my immediate urge to explode it would do nobody any good and might push her over brink. Calm thinking would be more difficult but more useful.

On consideration, I decided that there was little or nothing to be done late on a Saturday evening. Except . . . 'Did you also give them your credit card details?' I asked her.

She blew her nose violently. 'No. At least I had that much sense,' she said shakily. 'I knew nobody could possibly need both.'

Well, thank God for one small mercy. No need to hang about, cancelling credit cards and wondering when the accounts for diamond necklaces would come back from Hong Kong. I fetched a large brandy from the sitting room, encouraged her to drink it and then told her to go to bed. 'I'll make your excuses to your guests.'

'But what are they going to think?'

'They'll think that you're pregnant,' I said.

She managed a shaky smile.

I brought Joanna from the kitchen, where she and Mary were busily feeding dishes through the washer. Joanna took her mistress upstairs, promising to give her a sleeping pill and put her to bed.

I rejoined the party. I had never felt less like a celebration. From the far end of the table, Duncan looked at me anxiously. I gave him a nod and the kind of look which could have meant anything.

The absence of the hostess did little to speed the guests. It had been a good day and nobody wanted it to end. The aftermath of the dinner seemed to go on for ever. It had never been the custom of the house for the ladies to withdraw – Her La'ship would never have countenanced being excluded from the port and gossip. I managed to keep up some sort of conversation while my mind raced around the financial implications of Elizabeth's folly. I had put a lot of time and effort into consolidating Peter's rambling estate and business interests into a more compact package that would be easily managed by an heiress who was coming to it afresh. Knock a large sum of money out of the middle and it would be like knocking one stone out of an archway. The whole structure might not collapse, but it would certainly totter. Echoing her own words, I wondered how she could have been so stupid.

Joanna came in, on the excuse of renewing the supply

of cream for the coffee, to mutter that Elizabeth was asleep.

At last, somebody stirred and by common consent the guests rose to go, leaving messages of concern for Elizabeth. Ronnie emerged from the gun-room to hand each freshly cleaned gun, in its bag or case, to its rightful owner along with a brace of pheasants and to accept, with an expression of pleased surprise, a tip.

Keith and his daughter managed to hang back. As I supposed, an indulgent atmosphere among the guests suggested that most of them had leaped to the conclusion that Elizabeth was in an 'interesting condition', but Deborah had seen Elizabeth's face and she would have had to be a much less intelligent person not to have guessed what was afoot. We exchanged a few words in whispers.

'When does Ian get back?' I asked her.

She handed her gun-bag and her brace of birds to her father and dusted off her hands. 'He may be home by now,' she said.

'Ask him to come up in the morning?'

'Of course,' she said. They slipped out on the heels of the other guests.

Freed from his duties as a host, Duncan was on the point of dashing upstairs to his wife, but Elizabeth would not have appreciated being woken for an inquisition. I was fainting with weariness myself after all the fresh air and excitement, but I took him firmly into the sitting room, dispensed some more of his own brandy and gave him a summary of the bad news.

Duncan, to his credit, had never regarded Elizabeth's fortune as having more than peripheral interest for himself. It contributed some comfort to his lifestyle and saved him from having to worry about what the bank manager might say, but beyond that point his attitude was one of polite disinterest. His reaction was compassionate. 'Poor kid!' he said softly. 'I'll go up.'

'She's asleep,' I told him.

'When she wakes, she'll need me. There's nothing we can do just now and no more damage to be done.'

'That would seem to be true.'

Beatrice Payne had already gone up. Mary, Ronnie and Joanna must already have been on their way home and my fellow guest had made short work of his preparations for bed, because the rest of the house was dark and silent.

I wasted the minimum of time on my own ablutions. Tomorrow would be another day and a fraught one.

For what seemed like an hour but was probably only a third of that time, I lay awake and fretted. My old friend had trusted me. I had allowed his granddaughter to take on responsibility for her own affairs more rapidly than she could cope with and the result was a serious upset to the equilibrium of what he had left behind. For this, my fellow executor must take half the blame and I would make damn sure that he knew it. Ralph Enterkin, for reasons which I suspected were no more than laziness, had always advocated leaving Elizabeth to make as many of her own decisions as possible.

Despite my mental turmoil, a day in the fresh air and a vinous evening had taken their toll and I fell into a deep sleep. I woke at dawn. After a little thought, I decided that the steps to be taken financially were already clear-cut and that I did not know enough about information technology to make any useful contribution to discussions of how and who and where. With no demands on my thought processes, I dropped easily back into sleep.

The sound of a small car spurting away along the gravel woke me later. There were small sounds downstairs. The staff having worked late, it was to be a do-it-yourself morning. I showered, shaved and dressed and descended the stairs. I had not expected Elizabeth or her husband to have much appetite for breakfast, so I was surprised to detect the smell of frying bacon; but in the kitchen I found the pair sitting over mugs of tea and staring balefully at the back of the only other overnight guest, another remote cousin of Duncan's relative the Earl of Jedburgh. My fellow guest – a former professional man named Claythorpe, now retired from some unspecified vocation – was busily preparing a substantial cooked breakfast from ingredients which had been left out for the purpose.

Lured by the delicious smell I was tempted to await my turn at the frying pan. But I am careful of my weight – not out of vanity but for fear of being trapped in the older man's vicious circle. The heavier you are the less you walk and the less you walk the heavier you become. That was not for me. I put a single slice of bread into the toaster and helped myself to cereal and tea. Elizabeth kept catching my eye and sending unreadable messages. I had never before seen her with dark shadows under her eyes. Only good manners seemed to be preventing the couple from deserting their guests.

Clearly Elizabeth wanted to bend my ear – but, quite rightly, not in the presence of Mr Claythorpe. During my days in banking, one of the first pieces of advice which I would hand out to anyone who would listen, immediately after 'Remember, nobody ever calls you back,' was 'If you're in the financial mire, buy a new car.' The appearance of financial stability is essential. As soon as a rumour spreads that cash may be in short supply, every creditor wants to get in first to cream off as much as possible of what is due to him and every supplier wants payment up front, thus precipitating exactly what they feared. Immediately the word spreads, money is going out faster than it dribbles in and, if there was no cash flow problem previously, there soon will be. Credit is only given to those who have no need of it.

Mr Claythorpe took his time over breakfast. Conversation was understandably stilted but breakfast after a big party is not usually notable for bright chatter. I decided that he was not noticing anything special in the air. He finished at last. Ronnie must have made an unheralded early return to the house because Mr Claythorpe was pleased and surprised to find his bags already packed and waiting for him in the hall. He said all the polite things that a departing guest must say but then added to Elizabeth, 'Try not to worry, my dear. I'm sure that it'll come out right.'

Elizabeth made a small sound that might have been 'What?'

Mr Claythorpe smiled vaguely. 'My dear, I saw your face when the subject of e-mail fraud came up. Obviously, you've been taken. Not for too much, I hope. Just think of it as a useful tax loss. I'm sure that Mr Kitts can bring you out on the right side. I've seen him at work before.'

With that for a farewell, he pottered out to the last car remaining on the gravel, an old but gleaming Mercedes, and drove carefully away.

'I don't remember him,' I said. 'What did he do?'

'Something senior in the Inland Revenue,' Duncan said. 'I forget just what.'

'Maybe he has a point,' I said. 'But let's hope that it doesn't come to that.' I looked up at the kitchen clock. 'Where's Ian Fellowes got to?'

Chapter Three

Now that we were free to do something, however futile, about the missing money, Elizabeth and I were in a fever to get started. Even Duncan, who had never been known to get in a fever about anything, looked at his watch and raised his eyebrows.

Elizabeth went to collect the cordless phone and telephone a reminder but, Sod's Law being what it is, Ian's privately owned hatchback turned in under the big arch a few moments later. But by that time Elizabeth already had Deborah on the phone and, because Ian's wife is not one of the very few women capable of holding a short conversation, it was necessary for us all to wait while Elizabeth was again thanked for her hospitality, commiserated with over being taken in and treated to several stories about Bruce's early attempts at speech before she could disengage without giving offence. By then, Duncan had admitted the Detective Inspector and we had shaken hands very formally. Ian was making it clear that he was on business and not a friend for the moment.

'The study, I think,' Elizabeth said, turning in that direction.

I had been waiting to lend moral support and perhaps to intervene if, as so often happens, a feeling of guilt and inadequacy turned into rage at the nearest potential victim. With Ian's arrival, that danger seemed to be past. 'You don't need me,' I suggested. The truth is that my mind was sluggish and I wanted to excuse myself from a discussion which was bound to be long, boring, fretful and largely incomprehensible.

But Elizabeth deposited the cordless phone on the hall table with unnecessary violence and looked at me in surprise. 'Of course we do.'

'I can barely send an e-mail. I won't understand one word in three. You tell me the outcome and I'll help to deal with the financial consequences.'

'But you're my trustee.'

'And as such,' I pleaded, 'I need to make sure that we can get bridging finance without being scalped. And I should consult my fellow trustee.'

'You won't manage anything on a Sunday,' Elizabeth said firmly. 'And you know that Mr Enterkin won't be getting out of bed before midday. If then.'

At about that time, Hamish would have been sweeping the ground with the two dogs in case any pricked birds had been missed by the pickers-up and I would much rather have been with him, walking off the fumes of the previous evening and taking pleasure in the happiness of the dogs in their work. But Elizabeth had cut the ground from under my feet. I followed meekly into the study. This, if you discounted the computer, fax machine, two printers, an answering machine, several telephones and a small charging rack with three mobile phones on charge, was the traditional study of a wealthy and old fashioned gentleman, which was exactly what Peter Hay had been. Such of the walls as were not book-lined were panelled in pale oak and embellished with sporting prints. The chairs were deep and comfortable.

Ian Fellowes was a typical lowland Scot, stocky and sandy-haired. He listened in silence to the story of the disaster as related by a shamefaced Elizabeth and read through the copies of the two e-mails which she had run off for him.

When she had run out of both facts and regrets, he said, 'You can stop reproaching yourself. Older and wiser heads than yours have been taken in. I could name a few names which would surprise you but I won't – people are sensitive about their mistakes. The fact remains that anyone, caught by an apparently routine matter in a moment of distraction, can be fooled. Fraud would be impossible otherwise. You weren't expecting trickery so you fell for it. You'll be more careful next time.'

'That's for sure,' Elizabeth said gloomily. 'I was in the middle of form-filling for the tax man and my first reaction was *another damn form to fill in*. But that doesn't obscure the fact that I've virtually given away the price of a good farm. What are the chances of our ever seeing the money again?'

Ian looked sad. He was one of the many officers who hated above anything else the duty of breaking bad news. 'Not very good, I'm afraid,' he said. 'In fact, I wouldn't put them higher than negligible. I've just come back from a course on electronic fraud. E-mail fraud came high on the agenda and this series in particular took up an hour. Yours seems to be part of the same series – the wording within the message looks identical and is the same as the one that Mr Kitts brought from Edinburgh. It's been going on for two years now and it seems to be the work of a sophisticated person or syndicate.'

'Sophisticated, but not wholly familiar with the English language,' I suggested.

'That tends to be less noticeable in the Americas,' Ian pointed out. 'They operate almost entirely over the phone lines. The British end of the investigation is in the hands of the Serious Fraud Office and they're in touch with police forces throughout the civilized world, but it all takes time during which tracks can be covered. Look at it this way. In Britain at least, anyone can open a bank account over the phone. You give a name, get a password and a code number and that's about it. You deposit a sum of money in it and arrange for the Internet accounts to be paid by direct debit. You never touch that account again.'

He stirred the two pages with his finger. 'You send out these e-mails from anywhere and pick up the replies ditto. There's no law against adopting "CompuServe at Something-or-other" as your e-mail address. There should be, but there isn't. And you'd think that somebody at the Internet would insert a program to screen out such obvious attempts at fraud in the name of one or other of the service providers, but they haven't yet although I understand that it's in hand. Right, then. You set up a dozen other bank accounts – many more than a dozen in the States, where large transactions have to be reported – and use the BACS to transfer money from the account of anyone rash enough to respond.'

'What's the BACS?' Elizabeth asked him, frowning. 'Something to do with the Internet?'

Ian looked stumped for the moment. Evidently his course had not been as thorough as he was making out. I decided to help him. 'Nothing to do with the Internet,' I said. 'It's your telephone banking. The initials stand for

Bank Automated Clearing System, if that's of any interest. In Britain there's an office block full of computers – in Reading, I think.'

Ian tried to look as though he had known all along. 'Thank you,' he said.

'These people have to come out of the shadows and make contact with the money at some point,' I pointed out.

Ian nodded. 'Using the same system, they'll move the money around – probably to somewhere like the Cayman Islands, which is where a lot of the drugs money gets laundered. Then, at the British end, it probably comes back to the Channel Islands and gets translated into something portable – bearer bonds or certificates of ownership of gold. It could be drugs or gemstones. It takes time to follow up such transactions that far. It can be done but it always turns out to be a waste of time. The Serious Fraud Office is constantly tracking these movements in the hope that they'll make a mistake at that point and leave a trail that continues onward, but it hasn't happened yet. Maybe it never will. The portable assets get brought ashore in a suitcase and re-deposited.'

'And if they ever do make a mistake?' I said. 'Will anything helpful follow on?'

Ian shrugged. 'If they do, we may see some arrests but we're very unlikely to find our way to more than a fraction of the missing money. And how do you prove that any, let alone all, of that was ever yours?'

'The lawyers would have a bonanza,' I said. Ralph Enterkin would think that Christmas was lasting all the year round.

We lapsed into a gloomy silence. Elizabeth, I could see, was building up a head of steam. It had been in the nature of her upbringing to believe that society was ordered, that the police were there to protect her and that the law would right any wrong that was done to her. It was a view bound to provoke rebellion in the young. In the past, when she had been at odds with her grandfather, I had heard her cry out against the ordering of society and advocate the disbanding of the police – making all the arguments that come so readily to rebellious youth. But now that she had been dragged into the Establishment, it seemed that the ordering of society should be protecting her but had let her down.

'Take it easy, my dear,' I told her. 'It isn't the end of the world and you'll still be a wealthy young woman.'

'Just much less wealthy than before,' she said bitterly.

'I'm afraid that's true. But we must do what we can to minimize your loss.'

I had inadvertently offered myself as a target. 'Oh, do try to talk sense!' she snapped. 'How can you minimize a fixed sum?'

It hardly seemed to be an occasion for a detailed explanation of all the possible consequences. 'Imagine this,' I said. 'You're in a room. This room, if you like. Somebody throws a stone through the window. The glass has gone for ever, but do you let the stone bounce around among these expensive machines or do you try to catch it before it does any more damage?'

Elizabeth sat still while colour washed through her face. Then she nodded slowly and I saw her muscles relax. 'I'm sorry,' she whispered. Apology had never come easily to her.

'I can't help you with your damage limitation, I'm afraid,' Ian said. 'I'll take this copy along. There won't be anything I can do today. The automated parts of the system will be at work but people will be in short supply. I'll fax these to the Serious Fraud Office, first thing in the morning, and I'll let you know what if anything comes out of it. But don't expect to hear anything very soon. It's a slow business, tracing these transactions through places where there's a tradition of banking confidentiality, and there may be dozens of cases ahead of yours in the queue.'

'In fact,' Duncan said, speaking for the first time, 'the news won't be good and it won't be soon.'

Ian got to his feet. 'That's about it,' he said. 'I'm sorry to have to be the one to tell you this, but you might be wise to act on the assumption that there won't be any, ever.'

Ian could see that we had more than enough to be going on with. He made a quick escape. Elizabeth went with him to the door.

'Don't be too hard on her,' I told Duncan while we were alone. 'Go on being supportive. Anybody could have been fooled.'

He looked surprised that I should even say such a thing. 'It's entirely her money,' he said. 'She can give it to the Sally Anns if she likes. I'd miss my comforts but we would survive, so I'm not going to criticize. She can do that to herself, more and better, if we don't stop her.'

I had to agree. 'That's the other danger, permanent loss of confidence.'

'You can help there,' he said. 'Keep her occupied with other estate business. Let her see that she can make decisions.'

Elizabeth's financial well-being might still be my concern but I was damned if I was going to be solely responsible for her therapy. 'In case you'd forgotten,' I said stiffly, 'you're her husband. You should be able to nurse her through the bad times. That's what husbands are for.'

'I'll be nice to her,' he promised. His voice, as usual, was very calm, his manner laid-back. 'But the rest is very little to do with me. I have my own business – thanks, I admit, to a loan from the estate. My finances are quite separate and I prefer to have it that way. It's my job to support her.' He met my eye squarely. 'It's not a job I have a chance to shine at for the moment, for reasons beyond my control. If the worst ever came to the worst I'd do it, happily. But while Elizabeth still has money I don't want to take any responsibility for it. It would make me feel like a parasite. If I have to be one, I don't want to feel like it.'

Put like that he made it sound quite noble, but I had more than a suspicion that he was opting out of a process which was going to be both exhausting and emotionally draining. The devil of it was that I couldn't think of any valid counter-arguments.

'Until Ian reports back,' Duncan said, when Elizabeth returned and settled in the chair behind the big desk, 'there won't be anything useful to do except the damage limitation exercise. I'll scram out of the way and let you and Henry get on with it. I'd better go to the shop. I have a computer in with a faulty disk drive and the customer wants it back tomorrow morning without fail.'

Elizabeth nodded vaguely. 'All right, dear,' she said.

Duncan jumped to his feet and got out of the room before she could change her mind. He threw me a guilty look over his shoulder before the door closed.

'Uncle Henry,' Elizabeth said dismally, 'what are we going to do?'

I needed time to think. During Ian's visit I had heard Beatrice Payne's little car zoom up to the door and to my relief she chose that moment to bring in a tray with coffee. Noticing three cups, I was afraid that she intended to join us and I prepared to hint that matters confidential were to be discussed. But she only asked whether Duncan was coming back, which Elizabeth answered with a quick shake of the head. Miss Payne removed the extra cup and left the room with a lack of curiosity which, taken with her unusual reluctance to intrude, surprised me. She must surely, I thought, have detected that something big was in the air. Either that or she had made a guess, accurate or not. Or perhaps she had distractions of her own. I thought that she had looked less discontented, even hopeful. Perhaps she had begun to look forward to motherhood. It seemed more likely that the mysterious boyfriend had reappeared and supplied a dose of the loving which had been missing from her life.

Elizabeth managed to pour coffee. I accepted my cup from her before the nervous tremor in her hand caused her to spill more than a drop or two. 'First,' I said, 'an overview, so that we can be sure that we have the same understanding of our situation.

'Your grandfather had two priorities. Firstly, to preserve the estate and, secondly, to relieve the danger of unemployment in the area. As I understand it, you approve of both those aims?'

'Yes, of course,' she said impatiently.

'No compromises?'

'Definitely not.'

'Right. The two may sometimes be in conflict, but

we've been doing our best. With those aims in mind, we've been consolidating the estate. Talisman Farm was irrelevant and fifty miles away so we sold it. There was a better use for the capital.

'I suggest that there's no question of selling any more land.'

'Definitely not,' she said. 'We have a tidy boundary at last and it's all sort of interdependent.'

'Even if you were prepared to dispose of parts of the estate, this would be a terrible time to sell. We only got a good price for Talisman Farm because some of the land was needed for an extension to the industrial estate. In addition to the farms and forestry, there are several buildings in Newton Lauder. Most of those Sir Peter acquired as a result of trying to prop up businesses which were in danger. One or two could now be sold without endangering those businesses. That might make some small contribution to the equation. I'll have the factor look into it.

'Sir Peter also had investments in a number of local firms. We'll have to see if any of those investments can be sold without doing any damage.'

Elizabeth muttered something about drops and buckets but I let it go by.

'Now we come to Agrotechnics. Sir Peter founded the firm with the intention of relieving unemployment in the area and it has been largely successful. The designers have farming experience and the engineers are practical men. The firm had grown to the point where a substantial expansion was due, which is why the new share issue was floated.'

Elizabeth straightened up suddenly. 'Not the only reason,' she said. 'The employment situation in the

Borders is getting worse.' She smacked her hand down on the desk. 'Employers are being forced out of business by foreign competition and by government policies which take no account of anything outside the towns and cities. As long as there are jobless who *want* jobs . . .'

As a business philosophy, what she was saying might have been a road to ruin, but I was happy. I had not realized how closely she was following in Sir Peter's footsteps nor that she had even taken the trouble to think about the effect on local conditions. And she was recovering her confidence and poise.

I refrained from giving her a round of applause. 'Quite so,' I said.

She met my eye. 'Are you saying that I can't make the investment after all? Mary's cousin is out of a job and several others I know of.'

'I'm not saying that at all,' I told her. 'You have already made the investment, all but paying over the money. You're committed. You wanted to keep a controlling interest, so you underwrote a large part of the share issue. That has to be paid for in about three weeks' time. That's where most of the money from Talisman Farm was to go. Don't panic,' I added quickly as I saw her tense up again. 'You won't be led away in chains or declared bankrupt or anything. At a pinch, we could sell the shares again before settling day.'

'I don't want to do that if we don't have to,' she said quickly.

'No more do I, though our reasons are probably different. I want to keep the bulk of the shares in your hands to prevent a takeover by some rival who only wants to steal the technology and reduce the competition by asset-stripping the company. But, almost as important, you wouldn't get full value at the moment. I think that word has got around about Cowieson's difficulties. I noticed in this morning's paper that the price of Agrotechnics shares has fallen. We don't want to fix your loss.'

'And if Mr Cowieson pays up? Does that help?'

'It would be useful to Agrotechnics,' I said. 'The expansion could go quicker and easier. It's their money, not yours. But it might make it possible to negotiate a delay in settlement.'

She sighed and pulled a face. 'When I make a mess, I make a big one.'

'Always look forward, not back,' I told her. 'Learn from the past but think to the future. Regret never pays dividends.'

She stared at me for a second, puzzled and, perhaps justifiably, annoyed. I am inclined to pontificate at times. 'Surely,' she said at last, 'regret is always there?'

'Then give way to it for five minutes and then put it out of your mind and get on with your life,' I said.

'You're right, damn you, Uncle Henry!' She straightened her back. 'Well? What do you advise? What do I do?'

'Nothing about this for the moment. The ball's in my court, as they say. I had better notify my fellow trustee and speak to a few other people. You could clear your desk of the estate business that you wanted to see me about. Then you'll be available when you're needed.'

We filled in the hour before lunch taking decisions about a dozen matters of tenancy and finance. It would take her a day at least to gather the information and get the letters out. By then I could hope to have thought of some more tasks for her.

When we had finished, she came back to the problem of the moment. 'My grandfather had a heap of stuff from the other house stored in the outbuildings and the attics,' she said. 'Stuff which had come down from the ancestors. Junk, most of it, but somebody knowledgeable should go through it. A Rembrandt or two could come in useful.'

'Well done,' I said. 'That's the kind of thinking we need. There's a painting of foxhounds by John Emms in the dining room. It should make five thousand easily. Or does it have sentimental value?'

'None at all. I don't hunt and it was left to me by a cousin I didn't like very much.' Her rare smile had become rarer since the calamity, but she produced one suddenly. 'If it was Labradors instead of foxhounds, I wouldn't have given it up so easily.'

'Very understandable,' I said. 'I'll make an arrangement for getting things valued. Anything else?'

Her face fell again. 'Please God let something turn up! I had plans for the balance of the money. Roadside reflectors, for one thing.'

She had lost me. 'Catseyes, you mean?'

'Sort of. We've been getting too many deer killed and injured on the roads. Badgers, too. There's a type of reflector designed to reflect the lights of oncoming vehicles into nearby cover, to deter wildlife from coming out until the vehicle's gone by. The council have agreed to make a contribution.'

This was obviously something dear to her heart and, at a humanitarian level, I could see a great deal of merit in the idea. It would have been cruel to tell her to forget it. 'Put the idea on hold for the moment,' I said, 'until we see how it all shakes out.'

'It seems a bit hard that wildlife has to suffer because I was a bloody fool. And then, in the longer term . . .'

'Yes?' I said.

She hesitated and then it came with a rush. 'You were talking to Mrs Ombleby at the party last night.' She saw that the name meant nothing to me. 'She and Deborah Fellowes were the only two women shooting yesterday. You must know her. Well . . . This is in strictest confidence?'

'Cross my heart,' I said.

'Because if word gets around too soon, somebody else might jump on the idea. You know that computer shopping's coming in? You send in your order for the week and it's all gathered up automatically and delivered to your door. No need to struggle around a supermarket, looking for things that they've moved somewhere else since the last time you were in there, and queue for an age at a checkout. It's an infuriating waste of time.'

'I know about supermarkets,' I told her. 'I didn't think that you did.'

She grinned her old grin at me. 'I was a student for years,' she said. 'Sharing a flat in Edinburgh. I know all about supermarkets, thank you very much. But if you cut down on the time-wasting by shopping for a week, you've got the other bind of having to think about your menus for the whole week and listing everything you're going to need for them.'

'Isobel gets fed up,' I said.

'Most women do. So Mrs Ombleby thought, why not take computer shopping a stage further? Give clients a whole file of recipes, from the simple to the fancy, and a sort of table d'hôte standard menu for the week with umpteen possible variations. When you order you only have to list the meals and state for how many people. Then the right quantities of the ingredients are all packaged together and included in your order along with cooking instructions giving something else that most recipe books miss out – the number of minutes before the planned start of the meal for each stage of preparation to begin.'

'That,' I admitted, 'is clever. Ideal for the busy hostess or the career woman who's also catering for a husband or family'

'I thought so. It would be easy once the retailer's into computer ordering anyway. She's at the planning stage at the moment and talking to some of the better super-markets. She wants to try it out in Edinburgh and Glasgow and to be ready to go much wider if it catches on. That's when she'll need more capital than she can put her hands on. I wanted to invest in it.'

'It would need thinking about,' I said. And it did. I was thinking that I might sell a couple of my own pictures and invest in it myself.

Duncan returned for lunch although he was obviously preoccupied and impatient to get back to his workshop. Joanna served a soup and an otherwise cold lunch in a miraculously freshened dining room and left us to it. Mary and Ronnie, I was given to understand, were having the day off, in return for their long service on the pre-vious day.

Beatrice Payne came into the room as we began our soup. Duncan got up and pulled a chair out for her but she shook her head. She seemed withdrawn but there was still about her that air of expectation. Without sitting down, she dropped her own bombshell into our gloomy silence. 'You've been very good to me,' she told Elizabeth, 'and I wouldn't want you to think that I don't appreciate it. But I'm moving out.'

Elizabeth dragged her mind back from her worries. 'This seems a little sudden,' she said. She spoke mildly, as if afraid that any stronger reaction might provoke a change of mind.

'It is,' the other woman admitted. 'I feel terribly rude and ungrateful. But I've been offered a proper job at last and they want me straight away. It's not as if I'm much use here,' she added defensively. 'You wouldn't let me. You've been very tolerant but we've always known that it was a sinecure to save my face until I could find a real job.'

This was so close to the truth that it was difficult to find a polite denial although Elizabeth made a negative sound in her throat. To bridge an awkward gap, I asked, 'What's the job?'

'Office manager. That's what I was studying at commercial college. A friend of mine knew somebody who knew somebody,' she said vaguely. 'There's a furnished granny-flat I can have and I want to get moved in quickly.'

'But will you get your . . . holidays?' Elizabeth finished after a pause.

Bea actually laughed. Her spirits had undoubtedly risen and the sexuality which I had suspected was there to be seen. 'Maternity leave, you mean? We've agreed all that sort of thing and there's a crèche not too far away. When I'm settled in, I'll give you a call and you can come and give me your ideas about wallpaper and things.'

In deference to the previous evening we had been having an abstemious lunch, but Elizabeth got up and found a half-full wine bottle thriftily stowed in the sideboard and suggested that we toast Miss Payne's new job.

But that lady pleaded a dozen urgent tasks to be performed before she could move out and she left the room. Not long after, I heard her drive off, working briskly up the gears until the sound died away. She had left the room with a cigarette in one hand and an apple in the other. I wondered how she was managing to steer.

'Thank God!' said Duncan devoutly.

'You too?' Elizabeth queried. 'You never said.'

'Why would I interfere if you want to do a favour for a friend?'

'You're a doll,' said his wife. 'She did get under the feet a bit,' she admitted.

'She took note of everything,' Duncan said. 'I thought that she was sly. And always so dispirited. To tell you the truth, I was getting near the point of telling you that I couldn't take her much longer.'

Elizabeth threw him a glance so warm that it was almost indecent. 'And now you don't have to,' she said. 'I've been regretting what was really no more than an impulse, one of the things one feels that one has to say but not intended to be taken seriously. However, we've given somebody a helping hand and now she's on her way and we can try to get that part of our lives back to normal. Mary will be delighted – her nose has been out of joint ever since Bea came here. Are we finished?'

It seemed that we were indeed finished. Duncan went off in his car. I took a brief nap and then joined Elizabeth in the study. I had spent some time before lunch on the telephone, but Ralph Enterkin, local solicitor and my fellow trustee, would not be able to come and join us until late afternoon and nobody else was available who would be the least use to us in our present crisis.

'There's a message on the answering machine,' Elizabeth said. She pressed the play key. The rasping voice of Maurice Cowieson announced that he wanted to see me and unless he heard to the contrary he would pay a call during the afternoon.

It was a chance to give Elizabeth some easy responsibility. 'Blast the man!' I said. 'You see him.'

She jumped as if I had goosed her. 'Me?'

'Certainly. I saw more than enough of him on Friday, I don't want my Sunday spoiled as well. I've been promising myself a walk, to let last night's cobwebs blow away. You're just as much a director of Agrotechnics as I am and whatever we recommend to the board will go through.'

'But what's he going to want?' she asked nervously.

'He may want to give you a cheque, but I wouldn't count on it. More likely he wants to ask for more time to settle his debt.'

'And I tell him no way?'

'I'll go along with whatever you decide,' I told her. 'If you like, you could promise to recommend that we give him slightly easier deadlines. Go this far and not an inch further . . . Say, half by the end of the month, half the remainder by New Year and the balance at the end of January.'

She looked at me in surprise. 'Your quality of mercy seems a little strained,' she said. 'Why this sudden soft centre?'

'Gooseberry,' I said sadly, 'you give me too much credit. If you're going to push somebody into receivership, get as much out of them as you can before you have to start sharing with other creditors.'

'I might have known,' she said. 'But I thought he'd put up his business as security. Don't we have first call?'

'I hope so,' I said. 'And you can tell him from me that

if we see him doing something foolish, like paying off anybody else, we'll move in on him before he can blink.'

I left her looking thoughtful.

I changed my shoes for heavy boots, put on a cap, borrowed a stick from the hall and set off. As I had suggested to Elizabeth, I wanted to work a little well-being into my jaded old body. I was also hoping that exercise would work its usual magic and help my thoughts to sort themselves out.

The most convenient walks from the house all began with a crossing of the lawn behind the house to the wood beyond. From there, I found myself bearing towards Hamish's house. I had expected to find that the keeper was out on his rounds, but he was waiting impatiently at the game larder for the game dealer, who was already behind his promised time, to come and collect yesterday's birds. Spin, curled at his feet, looked equally disgusted.

We chatted for a while about the previous day's shoot. I might not have been so willing to interrupt my walk if Hamish had not seen and admired my performance. He was full of praise and I knew that it was not for the sake of a generous tip – he could be scathing about a poor performance or a breach of etiquette. I let him have his say. These little triumphs are too rare not to be relished. There was still no sign of the game dealer.

'I could wait for him if you want to get away,' I suggested.

Hamish brightened for a moment and then shook his head. 'Yon's a sleekit bugger,' he said, 'but he kens I've got his measure. I'd best bide here. But if you're looking to be helpful . . .'

'Anything I can do,' I said.

'Here's the way of it. Ronnie's awa round the west side with the Lab, to see if there's any birds the pickers-up missed yesterday and to check my traps for me. I'll dae the other half when the dealer's gone. But you mind the valley where we had the last drive before lunch? Och, but ye'll mind it fine, it's where you caucht yon broon troot last May. You could tak Spin an walk that bittie o the Den Burn. Ronnie's as sure as he can be that there was a runner not picked.'

That was about the right distance for me to walk. I said that I'd be happy to do it.

'An, while you're there, tak a look in the feeders an let me ken if they're low. An check the twa traps, either side of the feeders.'

'No problem,' I said.

'That'll let me get on.'

Spin, remembering some good days during his training, came with me willingly although he looked disappointed to see that I had no gun over my arm.

We took a different path, one that cut diagonally back through the wood towards the high archway, once the sentinel of an impressive group of buildings but now incongruously standing alone at the mouth of the drive. A small stream which passed through a culvert under the drive ran more or less parallel to the road but, as we followed it upstream, its rise was gentle whereas the road was comparatively steep. The result was that we were soon following the bottom of a narrow valley under a vault of tall trees, not yet bare of foliage but in full autumn glory. The ground on the other side of the road continued to rise, so that birds sent from there over the valley bottom were real 'archangels'.

The good weather was still holding despite the approach of a low from the south-west. It was a warm walk and I was glad of the cool of the season. In cold weather one can always add an extra sweater but during summer heat there is a limit to how much clothing one can take off but no limit to the assault of the midges on bare skin. The advice in the old song – *It ain't no sin / To take off your skin / And dance around in your bones* – may be attractive but it is hardly practical. I removed my cap to cool my head.

In many places the road was too near for safe and legal shooting, but in one place, where the stream and the road took opposite bends, the trees parted. The pegs for the previous day's stands were still in place. Spin, an experienced dog in spite of his comparative youth, knew what was expected of him and hunted the bushes with the bustling enthusiasm peculiar to spaniels. Most of the birds had returned to their sunnier and more favoured feeding-ground higher on the hill, but several came running out of the bushes and took off indignantly in front of the spaniel.

Further on, near to where I had caught the trout, we came to another glade where two feeders were raised between posts. I lifted the lids, but each was at least half full of wheat. With the stream nearby there was no need for a watering point. I followed narrow tracks and found Hamish's snares, both empty.

We could have turned back, but a wing-tipped bird might well have gone still further up the valley and I was enjoying my walk. I pressed on. The valley wall below the road became steeper, supported by broken rock. The bushes had closed in and walking was becoming more difficult, so I paused and sent Spin for one last hunt ahead. He plunged into the cover but came back out almost immediately. This might have meant no more than that there was no scent of a pheasant; but he was looking at me in a way that was different. I knew him of old and this was not how he would have reacted to a bird down a rabbit hole or dead but hung up in a tree. He was perturbed and uncertain.

I followed him, pushing between the branches of some overgrown rhododendrons. He moved away ahead of me, turning back now and again to be sure that I was following.

A splash of dark colour began to loom ahead. With a last effort, I forced my way through into a small clearing.

I was first aware of the smell of petrol. Then I made out a dark red car which stood on its nose against the rock wall of the valley. The engine was silent but there was still a hot smell about it, mingling with the odour of escaping fuel. The driver's window was fully open. The driver himself, I saw, was supported by his slowly deflating air bag; but his head was grotesquely damaged, so much so that I had to look twice to recognize Mr Cowieson Senior. There was no doubt in my mind that he was dead, but that was not for me to decide. Men had been known to survive appalling head injuries. I am still in touch with a former comrade who was shot through the head by a sniper, which cost him only the sight of one eye.

There was definitely nothing I could do for him. If some flicker of life still burned, I would almost certainly extinguish it if I moved him.

I took out my mobile phone. I only carry it in case I should suffer another heart attack while alone in the countryside, but it can be useful in other emergencies. I took a few seconds to recall how to use it.

Something was moving against my leg. I looked down. Spin had returned to his trade once he had passed the buck to me. The antics of men and cars meant little to him. There were more important things in life. He was trying to hand me a dead hen pheasant.

Chapter Four

I alerted the emergency services and took another and more careful look, in case the first paramedics on the scene should disturb vital evidence. Evidence of what I could not have said, but I was conscious of an uneasy feeling. The driver seemed to have been alone and there was nothing loose in the car except for a map and some toffee papers. I tried to memorize the details of the scene and then retreated, away from the smell of petrol. I had turned the ignition off but there might easily be a short somewhere.

There was only one useful function left to me. Retracing my steps, I found a place where, without issuing too open an invitation to another heart attack, I could struggle up the embankment. The road was always quiet but early on a Sunday afternoon, with an important Rugby World Cup match on the television, it could have been on the moon. The place where I thought the car had gone off was unfenced and any tyre tracks in the rough verge were barely discernible, but there was torn earth at the very brink and when I looked down I could see the rear of the car – shiny, bland and apparently undamaged. Spin sat patiently at my feet.

The ambulance and the first police car arrived together, driving away the silence. I waved them down, pointed out the wreck and the possible route down to it, and gave my name and temporary address. The officers looked curiously at the pheasant in my hands but decided that if I was resident at Hay Lodge the question of poaching was unlikely to arise. My duty done, I felt free to leave the scene quickly, before they remembered the long-standing tradition of keeping any possible witness standing idly, indefinitely and unnecessarily by.

It seemed a long walk back by road and through the archway although it was less than a mile. Spin made it clear that he did not appreciate being kept strictly to heel on the roadside verge instead of being allowed to continue raking through the undergrowth.

The elderly but shining car belonging to Ralph Enterkin, my fellow trustee, was already at the door of the house, so Hamish would have to wait for my report and the return of his spaniel. I delivered Spin and the pheasant to the kitchen, took a minute to wash dust and leaf mould off my hands and followed Ralph up. He was installed in solitary state in the sitting room with tea and biscuits. He looked up as I came in and his expression made it clear that, in typical lawyer fashion, he reserved to himself the privilege of keeping others waiting. He was a stout little man with a face which, usually jolly, could turn irascible in an instant, but we had worked well together.

I settled in the adjacent chair. 'I'd have been here an hour ago,' I apologized, 'but something happened. We have problems.'

He registered my lack of the usual courtesies and took in my appearance, distinctly dusty from my climb up to the road. 'So it would seem. In what area are these problems?'

'Twofold,' I said. 'We'll take them one at a time. I wanted this meet to tell you that young Elizabeth has been swindled.' I led him through the sequence of events very gently, but I could see that he was having difficulty in following. He was the least computer-literate person I had ever met and compared to him I was Bill Gates in person.

'Let me see if I understand you,' he said when I had ground to a halt. 'Somebody, by means that I shall make no effort to understand, requested confidential banking details which our ward was rash enough to furnish? And armed with that information the person or persons removed from the estate's current account the entire sum accruing from the sale of Talisman Farm?'

'Rather more than that. There was about two and a half thousand in the account before she made the deposit.'

'Oh dear!' Ralph said with remarkable mildness. 'And the money has gone beyond recall?'

'It looks that way. It seems to be part of an international series. Other instances are being investigated by the police, in London and elsewhere, without any real success. Ian Fellowes is going to have our case added to the others. If it turns out that ours is among the biggest losses, we may go to the front of the queue. But the chances of recovering anything would seem to be very slim, if that.'

'And there's nobody whom we can sue on grounds of negligence?'

'She could sue herself.'

Ralph considered the idea for a few moments. To a lawyer, the idea of unnecessary and hopeless litigation has a certain attraction. Reluctantly, he pushed the idea aside. 'This is not an occasion for levity,' he said stiffly.

He always regarded heavy-handed humour as his own perquisite.

'Nobody else is to blame except the criminal,' I said. 'And I suggest that you refrain from rubbing Elizabeth's nose in her folly. She has been calling herself all the names under the sun since we discovered the loss and she needs her confidence bolstered rather than damaged further.'

He nodded wisely. 'I understand,' he said. 'And it would shortly have been her own money, to dissipate as she saw fit. I may look at her askance, whatever that means – I shall probably have to practise in front of a mirror – but not a word of rebuke shall pass my lips. And what are we doing in the way of what I believe they call "damage limitation"?'

'I was doing some arithmetic this morning,' I told him. 'The stock market's still in one of its nosedives at the moment. Unless there's a shift in the market, the least expensive option in the short term would be to borrow at the most favourable rate I can find. I'm looking at other disposable assets. There are, for instance, a number of unwanted antiques stored about the place. Mostly bonfire material, I expect, but you never know.'

When deep in thought, Ralph was given to pursing his lips in a way that reminded me of a beginner learning to whistle. I watched, intrigued as usual, while he puckered up. 'You might,' he said at last, 'be able to negotiate a delayed settlement for the Agrotechnics shares if that agent – Cowieson, is it? – were to cough up. Let him be the one to pay interest. Or am I wrong?'

'You're right,' I said, 'but—'

Ralph was in no mood for buts. He waved them aside with an airy gesture. 'I'm told that he's on the way here and that he sounded quite cheerful. Perhaps he's raised the money. If not, perhaps the time has come for you to lean on him a little harder?' Ralph glanced at his watch. 'I must say that he's taking his time.'

'You'd better hear my other news,' I said. 'Where's Elizabeth?'

'Our ward and her husband went through to the study to try to make sense of their immediate cash flow. Wages have to be paid and bills settled. And the bank will have to be warned of any outstanding cheques, direct debits and mandates. Overdraft facilities will have to be arranged.' Ralph sighed deeply. 'There is going to be a great deal of extra work entailed,' he added as gloomily as though he was going to have to do some of it himself.

'So far,' I said firmly, 'we may only have scratched the surface. There is an added complication. I have been trying to tell you that Mr Cowieson will not be joining us. I found his crashed car an hour ago, with him inside it. I think we can safely assume that he's dead.'

This time, Ralph combined his pursing of the lips with a sharp intake of breath so that he produced a piercing whistle which surprised even himself. He blinked and decided to pretend that the sound had never happened. 'In law,' he said, 'the company remains unchanged and business continues as before. It would not be seemly, however, to foreclose instantly on his heir or heirs. Who would that be?'

'Probably his son, Miles.'

'One would suppose so. Speaking as one who acted on behalf of Mr Cowieson in more than one paternity case, I am not aware that he made a will; but he lived in his own little world, heedless of the consequences of his actions, and it would not be surprising if he had made bequests totalling far more than the value of his un-encumbered estate. My first guess would be that the Cowieson debt will take some weeks to resolve. Oh my God!'

'What?' I said.

'It has occurred to me that he may have made a will for himself on a form from the post office.'

'Is that so bad?' I asked.

'I have no objection in principle,' he said. 'It almost invariably leads to complications providing profitable work for my profession for months or even years. No, the fear in my mind was that he might, quite without my permission, have named me as his executor. Imagine the possible conflicts of interest!'

'You could refuse to act.'

'I suppose so. Ah well, it may never happen.' He blinked benignly at me. 'The debt is, of course, your concern as a director of Agrotechnics and reflects only indirectly on our problem with the Ilwands. Or is there any chance of Agrotechnics delaying its payments to the building contractor and giving us a little more time?'

'Not one single hope in hell,' I said. 'Read the Standard Form of Building Contract some time. That would be more expensive than borrowing from a usurer. I'll get us a better deal than that. How long do we want the money for?'

We spent the next hour going through the figures. To our relief, we found that Peter Hay's estate was incon-spicuously larded with disposable investments – shares in little known but profitable companies purchased as a gamble or as a favour to a friend, minor real estate, sporting rights to land long since sold. There were also the antiques which Elizabeth had told me were stored in the attic and outbuildings. The figures and timing were, for the moment, little more than inspired guesswork; but expressed as a discounted cash flow of the foreseeable income to the estate, even if it proved possible to dispose of only half those assets at realistic values, against the inescapable outgoings, the light at the end of the tunnel was not so very far distant. 'Right,' I said at last. 'We want to borrow half the shortfall for three months and the rest until July of next year. I'll get on to it tomorrow.'

'That's settled then. Now perhaps we should apprise our ward of what we have agreed.'

Before we moved through to the study, I phoned for Hamish. He did not answer personally – presumably he was doing his belated rounds or else still wrestling with his sworn enemy the game dealer – but I left a message on his answering machine. He must have come through his door while I was speaking, because he called me back before we had got to our feet. I reported on the one pheasant and the state of his feed-hoppers and traps and told him that Spin was awaiting him at the house. He would hear about the death of Maurice Cowieson soon enough.

In the study Elizabeth and Duncan were sitting before the computer screen, although neither seemed to have the spirit to look at it. There was an atmosphere in the room, as if the occupants were sick of talking, sick of each other, sick of life itself.

'Mr Cowieson still hasn't come,' Elizabeth said dully. 'He doesn't give a damn about keeping people waiting.' She shot a barbed glance at Ralph Enterkin. He was a frequent offender in that respect. 'Just for that,' she added, 'I'm going to knock a week off the time we were going to allow him for settlement.'

I realized guiltily that she would have been awaiting
the agent for several hours, quite unaware that he would
never arrive. I wondered how to break the news and
decided to be blunt. 'Don't blame him too much,' I said
at last. 'He made it almost to your gates, but there I'm
afraid he ran out of road. He went over the drop above
the Den Burn near where the Number One peg was
placed yesterday. I think he's dead.'

Her new responsibilities seemed to have induced a
softening in Elizabeth. She put aside her own troubles for
a moment. 'Poor man!' she said. 'And how awful for his
son! I must phone him.'

'I don't suppose that the son knows yet,' I said. 'He
was going to go away for a few days but, even if he's back
or he hasn't left yet, he may not have heard and you
wouldn't want to be the one to break the news. Leave it
until he's been informed.' My own feeling was that
Cowieson Junior might not be altogether desolated and I
might not altogether blame him, but there was no
immediate need to say so.

'All right. What are we going to do about it?'

'Nothing, until it's confirmed,' I said. 'Then we'll need
an Agrotechnics board meeting. He may not be dead. If
he's in a coma, we may have an even bigger problem.
But that isn't what we want to talk to you about. That's
Agrotechnics business and your problems are our more
immediate concern. We've been discussing how to bridge
the financial gap. I have some tentative figures here . . .'

We went over the figures in some detail with Elizabeth
and a reluctant Duncan. I was relieved to discover that
the miniatures hanging in the sitting room had no sentimental value but had been a bequest to Elizabeth from
an uncle who had bought them out of a house clearance.

With minor amendments, the figures were agreed and we drew up a list of assets. After some argument we also agreed who would make the opening moves towards the sale of each.

Elizabeth was still worried. She tapped my page of figures with a short but manicured fingernail. 'But what do we do about paying for the Agrotechnics shares until we can turn all this into cash? There's still a big shortfall. Will the bank give us that much of an overdraft?'

'They'd probably be delighted to,' I said, 'but the rate of interest would be crippling. Leave it with me. There's always money somewhere, put by for a deal that won't come off for a few months by somebody who'll be delighted if it earns a fraction over the bank rate.'

I would have been happy to expound for a little longer, now that we had moved into what had once been my field of expertise, but we heard the distant sound of the doorbell. Elizabeth got to her feet. 'I'd better go,' she said. 'Mary's on a day off and Joanna will be trying to cope with dinner on her own.'

She left the room but returned in less than a minute, looking flustered. 'It's Ian Fellowes,' she told me. 'Detective Inspector Fellowes, I should say – he's obviously on duty and there's another officer with him. They want to see you in private. Whatever have you been up to?'

I nearly laughed but it was not a subject for mirth. 'I found Maurice Cowieson's car down in the gully with him in it.'

She looked at me with her eyes wide. 'Oh. I didn't know that you'd been the one who found him. You never said. How horrid for you!' She gave a gentle shudder. 'I don't know what I'd have done if I'd suddenly come across a body, especially if it had been somebody I knew.

I've put them in the sitting room.' She looked at her watch. 'I suppose they're on duty, but help yourself to a drink if you feel like it.'

Ralph struggled to his feet from the low couch. 'I'll take my leave,' he said to me, 'if you don't want me to hold your hand and protect you from the bully-boys of the Establishment.' (Elizabeth flinched. She had once used that expression in the hearing of Ralph Enterkin and he had no intention of allowing her to forget it.) 'And I shall make enquiries about the sale of the properties in Church Street.' He managed to imply that he was undertaking the lion's share of the work before us.

I thanked Elizabeth hastily for the offer of the drink, excused myself and crossed the wide hall to the sitting room. Ian Fellowes was standing by the window. Instead of his usual tweeds he was wearing corduroys and a polo-neck and I guessed that he had been fetched away from his gardening. The very young man with him was more formally dressed but also in plain clothes. Ian introduced him as DC Brand.

'I can guess what this is about,' I said as we took seats. 'Maurice Cowieson.'

Ian gave me an affirmative nod and another to his companion, who produced a notebook and pencil. 'Suppose you tell us about it,' Ian said.

I gave DC Brand my name and home address for the record. 'Mr Cowieson was expected here,' I said. 'There was a message on the answering machine to say that he was coming. In fact, he asked to see me, but it was virtually certain that what he wanted to talk about was Agrotechnics business and Mrs Ilwand has an equal interest in the matter. She's as much a director as I am. As you know, her self-confidence got a bit of a jolt yesterday, so I left it to her to see him. I thought that conducting an interview while in a dominant position might reassure her.'

'Can we hear this message?'

'She erased it,' I said. 'I saw her. I'm sorry.' The atmosphere went from cosy to frosty. From his face, Ian was displeased. 'In future,' I said, 'you can tell us which messages are going to be vital information and we'll preserve them. Otherwise, they'll just have to take their chances.'

'All right,' Ian snapped. 'All right. No need to be sarcastic. I know that there was no attempt to hide evidence – it's just frustrating when such messages get wiped off. Did he sound drunk?'

I thought back. 'Difficult to tell from a recorded message over the phone,' I said. 'The phone does distort voices and he had that sort of harsh voice that doesn't express very much. On the whole, I think not. Or not very. You can ask Mrs Ilwand.'

'I will. Why was he coming? What was this dominant position?'

That question called for more thought. Financial affairs treble and more in importance from being bruited abroad. 'This is in confidence unless you really have to spill the beans,' I said. Both officers nodded solemnly. 'Mrs Ilwand and I are both directors of Agrotechnics. Mr Cowieson's business was retailing agricultural equipment and most of his business was in Agrotechnics products. He had built up a serious debt to Agrotechnics and had been given a deadline for reducing it. He claimed to be looking for financial backing elsewhere. He may have been bringing good news or he may have intended to ask for an extension of time. We don't know. Probably one or the other – and you may be better able to infer which as details of his business emerge.'

'If it's irrelevant we won't shout it from the rooftops,' Ian said, 'but I'll be amazed if it doesn't come out. Did his voice sound depressed?'

'Not that I noticed. Certainly not suicidal.'

Ian looked at me for a few seconds and then moved on. 'So you decided to leave him to Mrs Ilwand and then went and found his body. Not the first body that you've stumbled on around these parts.'

'The second – Sir Peter Hay's was the first,' I said. 'And neither of them from choice. He is dead, then? I couldn't be sure.'

'Yes,' Ian said. 'He's dead.'

'I thought as much. My arrival was quite by chance. You can ask Hamish.' I explained how I came to be in the right place at the right time.

Ian could hardly have married into his wife's family without learning a great deal about shooting. He was now a keen member of the Calder family syndicate. I could see that he accepted my explanation. 'Tell me what you saw and did,' he said.

'It was the dog that led me to the car,' I said. 'He came out of the cover and I could see that he was puzzled and anxious so I followed him. The car was standing on its nose against the bank. The driver's door was still shut but his window was down. The driver seemed to be dead. He was lying forward against the still partly inflated air bag. His head was badly damaged but I recognized Maurice Cowieson. I could feel warmth radiated from the car's engine, so it had happened not long before.'

'Did you touch him? Or the car?'

'Only to put two fingers on his wrist.' I paused. There

was something else . . . 'Oh, and I turned off the ignition, in case of a fire. I couldn't feel any pulse. His injuries looked severe enough to be fatal, but you can't always be sure. If there was still any life, I knew that anything I could do on the spot might make matters worse. I used my mobile phone, called the emergency services and then found a place where I could climb the bank so that I could flag them down and point out where it had happened.'

Ian asked a few more routine questions but I could see that he was not expecting to get any useful details out of them. Then, suddenly, he said, 'You don't seem surprised to see me here.'

'I'm not,' I said.

'Why not?'

'I didn't like the look of it any more than you do,' I told him. 'I didn't say anything to your friends from Traffic. It wasn't for me to stir up suspicions. I could have been quite wrong and wasted a great deal of police time. Privately, I had my doubts. For one thing, there were no skid marks up at the road. For another, his air bag had worked; but even if it hadn't it would have been difficult to see how he had come by those particular injuries – he could only have hit his head against the pillar between the door and the windscreen, and that would have caught him higher up and at quite a different angle. Then again, there was almost no blood on his face. With that injury, he must surely have bled, if only a little.'

'So how would you explain the lack of blood?' Ian asked me.

'That's for you to explain,' I said. 'My own thought, for what it's worth, was that the pattern of bleeding had been wrong. He might only have bled for a second or

two, but it could be that during that time he might have
been lying in such a position that blood had run in a
direction incompatible with a car smash, so somebody
took a damp cloth to him.'

Ian looked at me unseeingly while he thought about
it and then he nodded. 'Up at the road,' he said, 'did you
see any tracks? It was some little time before the boys
from Traffic realized that the picture didn't look quite
right and, by the time I arrived there, the ambulance and
two Traffic cars had driven to and fro over the ground
and there was a recovery vehicle parked in exactly the
wrong place.'

'The tracks were very faint,' I said. 'The ground's very
hard, as you know. But I think they went straight ahead
across the broad verge with no sign of braking and no
attempt to turn.' A stray thought reached me belatedly. 'I
forgot to look and see whether the car was still in gear.'

Ian must have been thinking along the same lines.
He nodded again. 'It's an automatic transmission and the
lever was in D for Drive. He was coming down the hill,
then?'

'That's right.'

'So he'd have been driving towards Newton Lauder.
Where had he phoned from?'

'How would I know?'

'Never mind. We can get it from the *caller display.*'

'I'm afraid not,' I told him. 'Hamish phoned me after
that. You'll have to find out from Telecom. Of course, he
could have been coming from his home. He lives – lived –
with his son in a house that stands on its own just outside
the industrial estate where his business is, at the southern
edge of the town. There's a country road from near there
which curves round the top of the hill. The road past the

driveway here climbs up and joins the other road at the top. It makes a way here which bypasses the middle of the town.'

'The middle of the town would be quiet on a Sunday afternoon.'

'If he'd had a drink, he might not have wanted to pass the front door of your police building. Are we assuming that he was driving himself?'

'We're not assuming anything, but if there was foul play it seems highly probable that he was killed elsewhere and the driver was then picked up by an accomplice.'

'I think I'd have heard any other vehicle,' I said.

'You might have heard. But would you have remembered?'

'I think I would. I was conscious of the silence.'

'Another vehicle could have come and gone before you were within earshot.' Ian paused and sighed. 'You really should have said something to my colleagues from Traffic.'

I tried not to sound defensive. 'And have been kept standing there for the next three hours? I was confident that somebody else would come to the same conclusions. Or the pathologist would be dissatisfied. If not, if you hadn't sought me out by tonight, I was probably going to have a word with you.'

'Probably?'

'I might have decided that I was letting my imagination run away with me.'

'As it happens,' Ian said, 'one of the ambulancemen was suspicious, but not until the body had been taken up to the road. If any evidence has been lost or disturbed, I'm going to be very cross with you. Very cross indeed.'

'I shall try to bear your strictures with equanimity,' I told him.

Ian and his helper spent a few minutes closeted with Elizabeth while Duncan and I had a quick drink in the sitting room. Joanna made a fretful appearance, insisting that dinner would be utterly ruined if not consumed immediately; but when the two officers departed in Ian's official Range Rover the meal appeared on the table, less fanciful than Mary's cordon bleu productions but wholesome, appetizing and certainly unspoiled.

We were three to dinner. Beatrice Payne had made a trip to inspect the accommodation which had been offered to her as a perk of her new job and to unpack the first cases of her possessions. She had returned, Elizabeth said, with her two empty suitcases, less gloomy than previously and perhaps a little hyped up, but seeming a little daunted by the changes rushing at her. She had said that the flat seemed perfectly habitable. She had dodged any questions about her destination, promised to send a forwarding address, packed the remainder of her few possessions, thanked her friend quite fulsomely, and made her departure.

'Actually,' Elizabeth said, 'there was rather more real affection in her farewell to the two dogs, but I'm not complaining. I'm too thankful to be rid of her.'

Miss Payne disposed of, conversation naturally turned to the demise of Maurice Cowieson.

'Ian seemed very concerned about how Mr Cowieson's voice sounded,' Elizabeth said. 'Drunk or sober? Happy or depressed? I couldn't tell them. What did you think?'

85

If Ian was continuing to imply that the crash had been either accident or suicide, it was not for me to mention murder. That word would surface soon enough. But I had seen Ian in action and heard tales from Keith Calder. It was Ian's habit, whenever circumstances allowed, to represent any death as probably natural or accidental to his superiors for as long as he could get away with it so that he would be left in peace to pursue his own enquiries on his own patch. And I could guess that his superiors in Edinburgh would accept for as long as possible the fiction that there had been no foul play so that Ian could continue the investigation without being able to make demands on their overstretched resources.

'I couldn't help them,' I said. 'I don't think that you could read any emotion into his voice even if you still had the recording available. He was one of those people whose voices go toneless when they have to speak into anything mechanical.'

Elizabeth thought that over and then nodded acceptance. 'I suppose that's true. But Ian was very insistent on knowing why I erased the message. I told him that I *always* delete messages as soon as I've heard them, unless I've got a good reason not to. Otherwise the thing gets bunged up. Or else I have to listen to a lot of drivel before I can get to the latest call. But Ian couldn't seem to see that.'

'He'll have seen it all right,' said her husband. 'It's just one of the questions that he has to be able to show that he's asked, in case it turns out that you did it of malice aforethought.'

'Well, I thought that it was a bloody impertinence,' Elizabeth said with a touch of her old imperiousness. 'I asked him if he'd still be able to give enough time to the little matter of our fraud, but he said that a couple of phone calls would start that ball rolling and after that there would be nothing for him to do but wait. He didn't seem to be holding out a lot of hope.' She sat up and squared her shoulders. 'Frankly, I've reconciled myself to the fact that I've been stupid and that the money's gone for ever. I can live without it. After all, the rent from one farm after tax, in this day and age, isn't worth wringing my hands over and pining for.' She gave a mirthless laugh. 'It's not every woman that's been swindled out of more than a million quid. That should make a useful dinner table conversation-stopper.'

This saintly resignation might be one way to avoid stress but it was not in the spirit of determined action which I had been trying to foster. 'But the land?' I said. 'And the investment in jobs? And what you'll have to sell to fulfil your obligations? You may write them off but as your trustee I have to take a more serious view. Nothing's worth fretting over or pining for, I agree, but aren't those things worth a little effort?'

She looked at me with her old haughtiness. 'What effort? What could we do?'

'You're the two electronic whiz-kids,' I pointed out. 'If the police aren't going to get around to hunting for your money until your case gets to the front of the queue, maybe you should start doing whatever they'll do when they've cleared their backlog.'

Elizabeth gave me another of her looks but decided to change the subject – for which I was thankful because I had only the vaguest idea of what I was talking about.

'I also asked,' she said, 'whether he'd thought to inform the next of kin but he said that they hadn't been able to reach his son yet. Ian implied that it was none of my damn business, but I have a business relationship with Miles Cowieson through Agrotechnics as well as knowing him socially, so I think I had a right to ask.'

'Miles spoke to me at the shoot,' I told them. 'He said that he would be going away for a few days. Or that he might go – I forget which. They've probably managed to get a message to him by now and in the morning they'll certainly inform the staff at Cowieson's when they turn up for work.'

'But if there's nobody there to take charge . . .' Duncan said.

'I've been thinking around that,' I said. 'I want to chase up some bridging finance for you and I can drive a better bargain face to face than over the phone, so I'll have to go into Edinburgh in the morning. It wouldn't be much of a detour to call in past the yard and satisfy myself that all's as well as it can be. If we're going to call up the floating charge in the near future, we don't want the asset to be deteriorating any further than it already has.'

Elizabeth nodded. 'I can't quarrel with that,' she said.

I was beginning to talk myself into a state of anxiety. 'When somebody dies or a firm goes bust,' I said, 'the vultures gather. Assets go missing. People seem to think that they're free to help themselves. I'll make sure that somebody's in charge and responsible. Can I have Ronnie to drive me? The prime advantage of having a chauffeur is that people lend you money more readily if you arrive behind one.'

Elizabeth and Duncan conferred silently. 'No reason why not,' Elizabeth said. 'Take the Range Rover.'

It was a generous offer but I had reservations. Sir Peter had been inclined to destroy his vehicles with ill-use and I would have known if a replacement Range Rover had figured in the accounts. 'Your grandfather . . .' I began.

They knew exactly what I meant. 'It's been resprayed,' said Duncan. 'And cleaned out. And there are new seat-covers.'

'In that case I'll be delighted to take the Range Rover.'

Before retiring, I made my customary phone call to Isobel. It seemed that they had continued to manage without my assistance. When I mentioned, as obliquely as I could, that I had found another body, her sigh came over the wire like the squall before a gale. 'So I suppose I'll be sleeping alone for another fortnight,' she said, 'like last time?'

There were too many answers to that one and none of them politic. It would be a brave intruder who faced up to Isobel in her curlers. To change the subject I told her, in strictest confidence, of Mrs Ombleby's venture.

'But that's brilliant,' she said. 'We'll have to subscribe.'

'I agree. I was thinking of selling a few pictures and investing what I can get for them.'

'I wasn't thinking of investment,' she said. 'I meant that we'll have to take the service.'

'I don't suppose they'll deliver outside Dundee.'

'They can put it on the bus and we'll meet it at the crossroads,' Isobel said.

Chapter Five

During the night, my worries subsided into something more worthwhile. I awoke in the morning to a feeling which was half-forgotten. It took me the several minutes while I brushed off the remnants of sleep to identify that feeling. Since my retirement, most days had been much of a muchness with few real demands on my time or mental energy. I had forgotten the Monday morning feeling, the awakening to realize that this was not to be another day of insipid rest but one for meeting challenges. I had almost forgotten about challenges but there had been a time when I thrived on them and some of the old zest remained. The first shock had worn off. I was stiff from the previous day's walking and concerned that I might have allowed Elizabeth to shoulder too much responsibility too soon, but the weight of years seemed a little less. I nicked my lip while shaving because I was trying to whistle at the same time.

The dark suit which I had worn for Friday's visit to Edinburgh seemed the obvious choice. I ate breakfast quickly and alone. The household had slipped into gear, by my standards, rather early. Duncan had already left for business and Elizabeth was pecking desultorily at the computer keyboard. Rather than break any concentration which she might have managed to summon up, I gave her a quick wave through the open door of the study. I phoned Gordon Bream from the sitting room and gave him a brief rundown of events. He agreed to keep the middle of the day clear for me.

Ronnie was waiting for me at the garage. He had added a chauffeur's cap to his everyday clothes, which I supposed was a step in the direction of the impression I wanted to make. Another and much bigger step was that the Range Rover was no longer the misused and scruffy vehicle which Peter Hay had left but now shone – and smelt – like new.

It was less than four miles to Cowieson Farm Supplies Ltd. The shortest route would have begun with a descent of the hill, but that route would have taken us through Newton Lauder at a time when the narrow streets would probably be full of traffic which would have included learner-drivers, cyclists, articulated lorries and farmers on tractors. Preferring a slightly extended journey with less risk to the Range Rover's renovated bodywork, I told Ronnie to turn right outside the arched gateway and set off up the hill.

At the place where Maurice Cowieson's car had crashed, a bend in the road had at some time been partially straightened, leaving a rocky embankment at one side and, on the other, a twenty-yard verge of compacted earth with weeds and coarse grass pushing through. The verge was already too much cut up by the recovery vehicle and those of the emergency services to show any useful traces so, on an impulse, I asked Ronnie to pull across the road and park roughly where I thought Cowieson's Rover had come to grief. My guess was good. When I got out of the car and looked over the brink, I was looking down on the crushed and broken bushes and a

91

puddle of oil where the car had landed. I turned to look back at the road. I was looking straight up the next section of road, which climbed for a hundred yards before the next bend.

I described the scene as I remembered it to Ronnie. 'What do you make of it?' I asked him.

Ronnie had spent much of his life as a stalker. He studied the ground carefully. The fine weather had given way to an overcast, but it seemed that he could make out signs which were hidden from me. 'I jalouse you'd the right o it,' he said at last. 'Gin the mannie suddentlie realized he was ower fast tae mak the bend, there'd be cahootchie left on the tarmac jist aboot here.' His gnarled finger described a line on the road. 'But mebbe he had a shock or a hert-attack?'

'It's possible,' I said. 'A pathologist told me once that a heart attack is an event, not a condition, and that unless an infarction lasts for some hours before death he wouldn't expect to find any signs of it. I'll tell you what bothers me. His seat belt was fastened and the air bag had inflated; but even if those hadn't saved him, I think the bash on his head would have been in a different place.'

For answer, Ronnie got back into the driver's seat of the Range Rover, lowered the window and leaned forward until his head was against the window frame.

'You're taller than he was,' I said, 'but this car's higher than his, so it would about balance out. Can you swivel your head to the right?'

Ronnie did his best, but no contortion that we could contrive brought the area of contact to where I had seen the wound in Maurice Cowieson's skull. 'Leave it,' I said.

'The police will have gone through all these steps. I just wanted to be sure in my own mind.'

Ronnie grunted.

Back in the Range Rover, we resumed our journey. No doubt Ian would have anticipated me but I kept an eye on the roadsides, watching for places where another car might have been parked.

The road climbed between tall trees for nearly a mile. Then it emerged at a T-junction onto open moor. We turned right onto an equally narrow country road, passing a house by the roadside – but Ian would certainly have enquired there. Our road descended through more moor, a corner of farmland, a cluster of houses and a small beech-wood. After two miles or so, the road brushed past a large house standing on its own beside the chain link fencing of the industrial estate and joined the old road south of Newton Lauder which still linked the town with one of the main roads between Edinburgh and Newcastle.

The house, a substantial dwelling of slate and granite which, long before the creation of the industrial estate, would have housed the family of a prosperous local tradesman, was almost hidden by a garden wall and a screen of trees, but there was no hiding the fact that the gateway was sealed with police barrier tape and guarded by a uniformed constable. I caught a glimpse of figures conducting a fingertip search in an otherwise neat garden transected by an open trench bordered by long heaps of excavated clay.

The gateway of Cowieson Farm Supplies was only a few yards along the road. The firm occupied a large corner of the industrial estate. It was not a major employer. Agrotechnics furnished the employment and Cowieson's Farm Supplies Ltd was one of the strategically

located firms the bulk of whose business was in demon-
strating and retailing the products of Agrotechnics. Even
the sales force was miniscule, usually comprising no
more than Maurice and his son. Other sales staff never
stayed for more than a few weeks because, I had heard,
Maurice Cowieson was in the habit of taking over any
sales discussions and thus robbing the salesman of his
commission. In a well-run business, many of the sales
would have entailed goods being despatched direct from
the factory but I was saddened and yet relieved to see
that the big yard, which should have held nothing much
more than demonstration machinery, was more than
adequately stocked. At least the assets were there. The
large warehouse building was presumably full. I could
see a yardman polishing a tractor but he did not seem to
be treating the task as urgent.

The smaller office block was fronted by parking for a
dozen cars, but only three spaces were occupied. One of
these was a red Mini. The main door, when I reached it,
was of teak, well made and expertly polished. It stood
open and I saw an inner glazed screen, also of teak. It
was a small matter but I sighed at the misplaced extravagance of the late Mr Cowieson. Farmers mistrust
expensive buildings.

The quality of the doors did not extend far into the
building. The entrance hall was large but plainly decor-
ated and severely furnished with hard chairs and a few
tables covered with brochures. Behind an equally utili-
tarian counter, a young girl was attending to some filing.
An older woman looked up from a keyboard. Her round
and unlined face had a cast of features suggesting patient
confidence but her expression was very serious. I recognized her type immediately, the devoted spinster who

can form the backbone of a firm, unnoticed by her employers and often unrewarded.

'Can I help you?' The older woman's voice was husky, as though tears had already been shed.

'Is Miles Cowieson in?' I asked her.

'I'm afraid not.'

'When will he be back?'

'We don't know. He decided to take a break. We think that he's abroad but we don't know where to reach him.' She paused and looked at me. 'I don't know if you've heard . . . His father . . .'

The younger woman sniffed loudly, to let it be known that she too was desolated.

'I had heard,' I said. 'In the absence of Mr Cowieson Junior, who is in charge here?'

The older woman looked uncertain. 'Well . . . I suppose . . . The office manager. We haven't had much time to make arrangements,' she added, apparently in explanation.

'Could I see the office manager, please? Say that it's Mr Kitts, on behalf of Agrotechnics.'

'One moment please.' She disappeared through one of the two doors which flanked the counter and re-emerged seconds later, holding the door for me.

There had never been an office manager at Cowieson's in the past. I was not altogether surprised when Beatrice Payne got up from behind a littered desk and came to meet me. A second desk which had been squeezed into the little office was starkly bare.

The receptionist closed the door behind me.

Beatrice Payne's eyes were moist, her lips were trembling and she was clearly in an emotional state. A visitor's chair had found a place in the crowded office but she did not invite me to sit down. As a result, we were forced to stand intimately close together. I was uncomfortably aware of her rather strong floral perfume. In all other respects she seemed to have changed her ways. She was wearing a smart business suit in navy with a sharply pressed white blouse and she had combed her fair hair from a frizz into tidy and natural-looking curls. The change into more formal office attire should have had a neutering effect but the sensuality of her body and body language seemed rather to be enhanced. Even my elderly hormones turned over in their sleep.

'Oh Mr . . .' She paused and embarrassment was added to her other distress. Evidently she had forgotten my name already. She took the easy way out. 'Oh, Uncle Henry! It's awful!'

'Death usually is pretty awful,' I said.

She waved a vague hand. 'That's not what I meant,' she wailed. 'Oh, I know it's awful, Mr Cowieson being dead and the police all over the place asking questions and saying that they aren't finished with us yet but not saying *why*. And there was a reporter here earlier, hinting at something mysterious, and a man who wanted money for an unpaid account that I can't find, and anyway I'm not empowered to write cheques yet. But Mr Miles is away, I don't think he even knows about his dad, and everything's upside down.'

'You'd better tell me about it,' I said.

She paused for a moment and then rushed on, evidently deciding that either as a director of Agrotechnics or as an honorary uncle I might be able to help. 'I was engaged as office manager. But you knew that. It was mostly at . . . at Mr Miles Cowieson's urging, but I think that Mr Maurice could see that it was high time things were taken in hand. They'd been trying to do everything between them, selling and bookkeeping and management and everything, with only a typist in the office and a girl to make the tea and an occasional salesman who never lasted long, and getting into a right old guddle, which didn't leave them much time for selling anything and made it difficult for either of them to get away for a holiday.'

She paused and took a deep breath. 'So Miles said that he'd take the opportunity for a break and go off for a few days or maybe a week and his father would keep me straight and he'd come back and keep me even straighter – that's what he said – but the police met me on the doorstep this morning – my first day! – and told me that Mr Maurice was killed in a car smash yesterday. Those two out there aren't any help, they just want to see me make a fool of myself. And I don't know what to do.'

A suspicion in my mind grew into a certainty. Whether or not Miles Cowieson was Bea's lover and the father of her child, he was certainly the friend who had recommended her for the post. Probably his father had been digging in his heels and Miles had been allowing time for the idea to sink in. But my suggestion that existing staff would be kept on if Agrotechnics took over the firm had triggered some hurried activity. If Miles and Bea were to count on working in cosy proximity, she would have to be in post before Agrotechnics took command.

I opened my hands in what was intended to be a vaguely supportive but non-committal gesture. Evidently she took it for an invitation to a comforting hug, because she swayed forward and leaned against me so that I was enveloped in her floral perfume. Other nationalities may hug comparative strangers at the drop of a hat but we Brits pride ourselves on a certain reserve. Besides, I was past the age at which I could get more than nostalgic pleasure from physical contact with a young woman. I could hardly push her away but I was damned if I was going to hug her. I administered a sympathetic pat on the back but when I tried to back away I found that I could only take half a pace before my back was against the partition and Miss Payne was still plastered against my front.

'Suppose we sit down and you can tell me what the problems are,' I suggested.

She took me up on the second part of my suggestion but not, unfortunately, the first. 'The phone's been going non-stop,' she said. Her brow wrinkled as she realized that it had not rung since I came in. 'It'll probably start again in a minute.'

'Then I suggest that you pick it up and tell the lady on the counter that you aren't taking any more calls while I'm here and that she's to get a number and you'll call whoever it is back.'

She produced the shadow of a relieved smile and did as I suggested. While she was dealing, surprisingly firmly, with the phone, I took the opportunity to step sideways and take a seat in the chair behind the vacant desk. I feared for a moment that, having adopted me as a father figure, she was going to sit on my knee, but she slammed down the phone and almost threw herself into the other desk chair.

'Now,' I said. 'Cough it up.'

The vulgar expression seemed to hit the right down-to-earth note. She set off again more calmly. 'Mostly, it's been farmers wanting to know the prices of things I've never heard of or wanting to be advised what we'd recommend for doing a certain job. I've a list . . .' She picked up a sheet of typing paper and frowned at it. 'I understand the paperwork all right, though it could be done much more effectively. I've even heard of the things they . . . we sell. I've found a price list and I think I can identify most of the things which are referred to by numbers, but I don't know if the list's up to date and I cannot answer technical questions. I could learn, but I'm not being given the chance.'

'Every enquiry must be followed up,' I said. 'No question about that. Is there nobody else here who can help?'

'Not a soul. There's a yardman who just keeps things clean and orderly, a storeman who knows what we've got but not what it's supposed to do and a mechanic who's off sick.'

'Then let's get you some help,' I said. 'Get me an outside line. I want to speak to the Agrotechnics factory.'

Facing up to tasks which were well within her competence had a further calming effect. She placed the call for me and transferred the connection to the phone by my hand. The girl on the factory switchboard knew me for a board member, so I was soon speaking with Cyril Jacks, the factory manager. 'We have a problem at Cowieson's,' I said.

'So what else is new?' he asked glumly.

'Not just the settlement of outstanding accounts. This is a newer and bigger problem,' I told him. 'Had you heard that Maurice Cowieson was killed in a car smash yesterday?'

We lost a minute or two while he expressed shock and asked for details which I furnished very sparingly.

When I felt that the discussion could decently move onward, I said, 'It's even more of a problem than that. Miles Cowieson has gone off on holiday. Nobody seems to know where and I don't suppose that he even knows about his father's death yet. There's a brand new office manager here and she doesn't know how to answer the enquiries that are coming in. Can you give her a name or names that she can contact for technical or financial information, so that she can call the enquirer back?'

He considered for a very few seconds. 'I can do better than that,' he said. (I breathed a sigh of relief. It was what I had hoped he would say.) 'It won't help anybody if Cowieson's gets into an even bigger fankle. I'll send my assistant over right away. He can hold her hand for a few days. Then, when she's getting the hang of it and if Miles isn't back by then, he can leave her with a price list.'

'She has a price list,' I said, looking at the other desk.

'Well, tell her that the prices are slightly inflated and she can give each farmer ten per cent off as a special favour, in confidence. Every farmer loves to think that he's driving a hard bargain and getting a discount that nobody else is getting. I rather suspect that old Maurice has been keeping the discount for himself, so that potential clients simply transferred their enquiries to other outlets. We've sometimes been getting orders for machinery to be delivered in this area but coming from other agents.'

'Small wonder that the firm's in difficulties.'

'Very small indeed. We're only a couple of miles away, so my man will be with you in ten minutes. You remember Colin Weir?'

'I remember him very well,' I said. I had been thinking

of Colin as a possible manager for Cowieson's if Agrotechnics had to take over.

I told Miss Payne that help was on the way and she looked at me as though my next trick would be to feed the five thousand.

It seemed to be a good time for frankness. 'I'm surprised that they took on an office manager at this time,' I said. 'Not that it isn't needed; it's long overdue. But did anyone explain to you that there are certain financial hurdles ahead?'

Before I had finished speaking she was nodding energetically. 'Mr Miles was very frank about that,' she said. 'He explained that they could only make it a temporary appointment for the moment but his father had agreed at last to let him pull the firm out of the mire and he was sure that he could do it, given some fresh capital. Between you and me, Uncle Henry – you don't mind me calling you Uncle Henry?'

'Not in the least,' I said.

'That's all right then. I'm so used to hearing Elizabeth call you that, and Duncan as well but not to your face, that I can't help it. I think that Miles is trying to raise the capital now. He put it about that he was going for a holiday, but I think that that's where he's gone. He let something slip.'

'He may not get anywhere,' I pointed out. 'But if you and Colin can shift enough of the stock to settle a substantial part of the debt, the whole situation might change.'

'That would be wonderful,' she breathed. 'I have a lot of hopes riding on this job. I took it on because I needed any job, even a temporary one, because it's much easier to get a job when you've already got one or just been

101

made redundant. But I must admit that I was really sold by being offered the granny-flat in the house. A place of my own with a nice garden – at least, it will be nice when they've finished replacing the lead pipes and put it back together again.' Her face was lit by an inner radiance and the beauty that I had once suspected burst out. 'I'll show it to you, some time,' she said, 'when I have it looking right.'

'I'll look forward to that,' I said.

Colin Weir, a thin young man with a wispy beard but a firm grasp of agricultural technology and economics, turned up within the promised ten minutes and after a little verbal sparring the two seemed to arrive at a cool understanding. I decided that I could safely leave them alone to work out a *modus vivendi* without any fear of battle breaking out.

That left me free to resume my journey to Edinburgh. Rather than risk the occasional congestion in the middle of the old town of Newton Lauder, Ronnie turned south for a mile or two until we came out on the main road. While we headed north again, I turned the situation over and over in my mind. Every effort to simplify it seemed only to add further complications. There were too many unknowns in the equations. Would Miles Cowieson find a source of money? Would he be as amenable to a friendly takeover as he had once suggested? Cowleson's must be losing money and goodwill hand over fist, but would a hostile takeover be in their best interests? And how would it best be accomplished? How were any other creditors affected? In the end, I decided that my immediate task was clear. I had to make sure that liquidity was available so that Elizabeth could meet her obligations. After that, each new fact would have to be dealt with as it emerged.

Having arrived at that much of a decision I was free to enjoy the beauty of the day but, unfortunately, the expected low had arrived and the fine spell had ended. Grey cloud had drawn across the sky. The heather-clad hills had turned a dirty grey. There was just enough of a drizzle to make smears on the windscreen but not enough to wash them away. Other vehicles managed to throw up a thin mush of mud and leftover rubber. Heavily laden artics pulled a trail of opaque mist behind them. Ronnie's patience and the washer-bottles were both exhausted by the time that we reached Gordon's office.

The second advantage of having a chauffeur (after impressing potential sources of finance) is that you have no need to park the car and then walk back in the rain from the remoter corners of the city. The third is that you need not worry about casual theft or vandalism. I gave Ronnie some money for a car wash and lunch and told him to go and find somewhere where he could keep an eye on the car while he ate and then sit in it. I would use my mobile to call him on the car phone when I needed him. Ronnie accepted these instructions placidly and I recalled that he had a sister in nearby Gogarburn who would no doubt be good for a free meal.

Gordon had at one time been my assistant but he was too much of a go-getter to remain in banking, where promotion is slow and uncertain. He had left to become a partner in an accountancy firm which had grown large under his nurturing, but not too large to be run efficiently and with due regard to every client's interests. Gordon himself was now far too senior to dabble with clients' accounts. Instead, he was a financial and taxation adviser of some standing as well as being a director of several companies. He had been known to say that his success was due in part to the early training which he had had at my hands. I was never sure whether he was sincere or ironic, but preferred to assume the former.

The firm had swallowed a large part of one of the tall, mostly Victorian crescents with which Edinburgh abounds and Gordon had retained for his own office one of the former drawing rooms, redecorated but otherwise unaltered, complete with the original plaster cornices and furnished in period except for the inevitable computer and telephones. It must have been one of the most comfortable and impressive private offices in Scotland.

Although I had made an appointment, Gordon showed a sign of surprise as he greeted me, evinced by a minute raising of one eyebrow. (Later, when I recalled that Ronnie had tried to hide a smile when I returned to the car, I realized that Bea Payne's floral perfume was clinging to me and I found a trace of her face powder on my lapel. To what conclusion they had leaped I could only guess, but I was not wholly displeased. At my age, reputation has to make a poor substitute for actuality.) Gordon ignored the big desk and led me to a group of deep chairs around a low marble-topped table. A secretary brought coffee. When we were alone, Gordon said, 'Now, Henry. What's the panic?'

'Panics,' I said. 'Plural. Did you know that Maurice Cowieson is dead? Found in his car at the bottom of a steep embankment. Found by me, incidentally.'

His eyebrows shot up and the habitual smile was wiped away. 'No, I hadn't heard. There was something on the radio this morning but it didn't give an identity.

The usual formula – "until next of kin have been informed".'

'Therein lies the rub. Next of kin – believed to be Miles – has gone off abroad, officially on holiday but probably chasing after fresh finance, and can't be contacted. There's a new office manager who only started this morning. Old Maurice was supposed to be inducting her, but he's not much help now – for want of a spirit guide. I've borrowed Cyril Jacks's assistant for a few days. He and the office manager can run the place between them. I'll keep an eye on the pair of them. By the time Cyril has to have the boy back, Miles may have returned with fresh money and everything in the garden will be lovely again. Or, of course, not.'

Gordon rubbed his chin. 'Or, as you say, not. Until then, it seems to me that you've done all that's possible. We'll have to wait. Play it off the cuff. Keep me posted.'

'There are other factors,' I said. 'There seems to be at least one other creditor.'

'That could be his bad luck. After all, we do have a floating charge.'

'Half a dozen others may think they're covered too,' I pointed out.

Gordon's nostrils flared. 'Cowieson's couldn't give another floating charge. That would be impossible.'

'But I can imagine several ways by which a gullible creditor could be tricked into thinking that he'd got some form of guarantee. In my opinion – feel free to disagree – old Maurice had just the right mixture of cunning and stupidity for that sort of double-dealing.'

'I wish I *could* disagree,' Gordon said, 'but I can't. Luckily for us, no guarantee would outweigh our floating charge. I checked it myself and then went along with our solicitor to see it registered in the Companies Register. And a limited company is a separate legal persona from its members and is unaffected by the death of its directors.'

'Unaffected legally,' I said. 'But liable to be very much affected all the same. Maurice was chairman and managing director and just about everything else. He managed to retain a majority of the shares in his own hands and had no intention of ever being outvoted – that, I suspect, is why he didn't find much-needed capital by way of a share issue. His son, Miles, is also a director but the old man kept him on a very tight rein. The only other director is a female, some sort of cousin I think, who lives in Troon. She supported Maurice all along the line.'

'Is Miles really the heir?' Gordon asked, frowning.

'I don't know yet. But it's probable. Now add to the equation – in strict confidence – that the police have grounds to believe that Maurice's death wasn't entirely accidental. I can't say more than that at the moment. I'll stay in touch and see what develops.'

'I think you're right,' he said after a moment's thought. 'No point rocking the boat just yet. Better to change my metaphor and see how the cookie crumbles. Let me think about it and we'll talk it out over lunch. Is that the lot?'

'I wish. You remember the e-mail fraud that you told me about?'

Gordon pointed out that our previous discussion had only been the previous Friday. So much had happened since then that it seemed more like a month.

'Elizabeth Ilwand had already been caught, for a large sum. In fact, for the price of the farm which we sold to provide for the investment in Agrotechnics, plus whatever was in the account before that cheque cleared. I hope and believe that it was coincidence that she was hit during the few days when the estate's current account was overflowing, but I'm keeping an open mind.'

Gordon tutted but wasted no time in mere commiseration. 'She can still complete the investment?' he asked keenly.

'No question about that. But it may take a little time to realize that sort of sum without throwing good money after better. I'm looking for the cheapest way to raise money in the fairly short term.'

Gordon looked at his watch. 'I've booked a table for lunch,' he said, 'but we have a margin of more than an hour. I'll give you a list of numbers to call while I consult my partners. With a bit of luck, I may find that we have a client in search of a short-term investment.'

A fourth advantage of having the services of a chauffeur is that of not having to worry about the breathalyser. We had a good lunch and I had the lion's share of a bottle of claret. I was in celebratory mood. The banks, insurance companies and pension funds had been overcome with greed at the prospect of a large, short-term loan and I had been forced to recognize for the thousandth time that almost the only honest way to wealth these days is to become good at something totally useless. For a while I was afraid that we would have to add to the wealth of a pop singer – one, in particular, whom I especially despised – but we tracked down among Gordon's clients a National Lottery winner who expected to take occupation of a substantial and expensive property in the early spring and would be delighted to earn a better rate of return than his bank was giving him until the day when he had to pay over the money. In addition to this success, I still cling to the belief that red wine is good for the heart.

All good lunches come to an end. Ronnie responded promptly to my phone call and carried me to an auction house where in the past I had spent a perhaps excessive proportion of my income. That at least was Isobel's view, although most of my investments had proved to be sound and several of the paintings had risen sharply in value. I remembered one of the partners and, to my surprise, he remembered me. His name was Stoep, pronounced Stoop, and since he had indeed a pronounced stoop I had no difficulty recalling his name, which seemed to gratify him. He was as tall and thin as ever but his hair had thinned and his black moustache was now grey. He took me into an office where there was barely room for a desk and two chairs between all the unsold detritus from previous sales – goods which owners were still to collect or had finally abandoned.

We exchanged a few courtesies but he was obviously waiting for me to get down to brass tacks. A stuffed but moth-eaten owl behind his right shoulder seemed to be holding its breath.

'You remember Sir Peter Hay?' I asked.

'Very well indeed.' I seemed to have caught his interest. 'I was sorry to read of Sir Peter's death. I remember – going back twenty years or more – when the big house burned and a lot of valuable stuff went with it. He bought some nice pieces through us for the new house. If his estate wants to part with any of them . . .?'

'Not those,' I said. 'But they also had the other family place up north for the salmon and stalking. When he sold it, he kept a lot of the better furniture and pictures. Some of it was quite unsuitable for the smaller, modern house, so what he couldn't bear to part with went into store. He may have expected his granddaughter to set up her own establishment while he was still alive.' I paused and chose my words with care. The wine might have loosened my tongue and any mention of a need for money is an immediate signal for the vultures to circle. 'They don't have the same associations for his granddaughter and she now owns Hay Lodge, so the time may have come for a clear-out.'

'I quite understand,' he said. 'Shall we have it uplifted?'

'We'd prefer to have a valuation first,' I said, 'just to be sure that sale value exceeds sentimental value. I wondered if you could send somebody . . . ?'

'I'll come myself,' he said quickly. He opened his diary.

I was able to enjoy the fifth and, as far as I am concerned, final advantage of being chauffeur-driven. I slept for most of the way back to Newton Lauder. I had told Ronnie to take me back by way of Cowieson's. I had to reassure myself that the business was in good, or at least adequate, hands and that no calamitous disputes were raging.

With more tact than I would have given him credit for, Ronnie switched on the car's radio as we neared the town and by the time we entered the industrial estate I had roused myself. Peter Hay must have had a similar need for an after-lunch nap, because Ronnie reached back over his shoulder with a box of Wet Wipes and a small flask of what turned out to be diluted brandy. Soon, refreshed inside and out, I felt rather more than my usual self again.

In front of Cowieson Farm Supplies was parked a Jaguar, showing some rust and at least one minor dent although comparatively new. In the entrance hall, Beatrice Payne had emerged from her office to confront a small man in a dusty suit who was brandishing some papers and seemed to be in a state of considerable agitation.

Miss Payne looked up as I entered and she seemed to brighten. 'Here's Mr Kitts,' she said. 'He'll sort it out.'

I was not sure whether to be flattered or annoyed by the assumption that I would wave some sort of magic wand, but she had left me no escape. 'Can I help?' I asked.

The man had a red and weather-beaten face, small, piggy eyes and a bristling moustache. 'Allardyce,' he said brusquely. His voice was harsh and remarkably deep for such a short man. 'McQueen and Allardyce, building contractors.' He brandished his papers. 'We put up this building and the Defects Liability Period is long gone. Forty-eight thousand outstanding and I'm not leaving here until I've got something very substantial on account.'

'Then your visit may be rather a long one,' I told him. 'There is nobody here just now with any authority to write cheques on the company's behalf.'

His eyes, not very wide in the first place, narrowed further. 'I know your name,' he said. 'Kitts. *She* told me. But who *are* you?'

'I'm a director of Agrotechnics. I think that you're doing a big job for us just now.' The girl and the secretary were listening, fascinated, so I kept it as discreet as I could. 'We have a larger debt to collect and we were granted a floating charge.'

'So were we,' he said triumphantly. 'And the company goes on even if the boss has died. I asked my lawyer.'

This was interesting. The media did not have the name of the deceased. 'How did you come to hear about a death?' I asked him.

He hesitated. 'Word goes around,' he snapped. 'Cowieson's were never good payers at the best of times and this won't make it any better. I've come to collect.'

Just as I had feared. Maurice Cowieson had pledged the business to two different creditors. 'Mr Maurice Cowieson died yesterday and Miles Cowieson is abroad,' I said. 'I think that we should discuss this outside.'

He looked at me sideways but evidently decided that I was not inviting him to physical violence. He nodded and we walked out into the car park. A cold east wind began to suck the heat out of me but I had developed a dislike of the man and I had no intention of being closeted in a car with him.

When I was sure that we were out of earshot of the building I asked, 'When was your floating charge granted?'

'Nearly four months ago.'

'Ours is nearly a year old,' I said. 'Even if they were both valid, which is legally impossible, I'm afraid ours would take precedence. Did you have a solicitor check the Companies Register and then register your floating charge?'

Mr Allardyce was looking slightly nauseous. 'He assured me that his solicitor had done all that on our behalf.'

'I'm afraid you've been taken for a ride,' I said. 'We –

Agrotechnics – are doing all we can to rescue Cowieson's with a view to taking it over if necessary, in which event you've a good chance of being paid. But Maurice Cowieson had no right to grant floating charges to two different creditors. In fact, it was legally impossible and the attempt was almost certainly criminal. His death makes that aspect of it irrelevant but on the other hand, as you said, the company still goes on. The fact remains that if you make a public stink, we won't touch it with a bargepole. We'll repossess as much of the machinery as hasn't been paid for, which is most of it, Cowieson's will go into liquidation and nobody will get more than about twopence in the pound.'

He could see the point but not the holes in my argument. All the same, he was reluctant to let go. 'Even something on account . . .' he said wistfully. 'We need the money to buy materials for your job.'

That isn't how the building business is financed and we both knew it. 'Your contract with Agrotechnics provides for payment for materials on site. Nobody was expecting old Maurice to drive off the top of an embankment,' I pointed out. 'The office manager only started this morning. As I told you, there's nobody here with the authority to sign cheques. When Miles gets back from wherever he's gone you can try him but, unless he's managed to raise some new finance, the likelihood is that we'll push for an agreed buyout immediately or, if we don't get a satisfactory deal, call in a receiver.'

He clenched his fists until the papers crackled and he walked slowly round in a small circle while he thought about it. 'The bugger!' he said at last. His red face had gone much the colour of a half-ripe plum. 'If he wasn't already dead, I'd kill him. You'll see that we get a fair deal?'

I was not at all sure of the law, nor whether Agrotechnics would go along with any promises that I made. 'I'll do what I can,' I said. 'I can only say that your chances of getting your money are very much better if you don't rock the boat just now.'

The fact that I hadn't given him any easy promises seemed to reassure him. He even shook my hand before driving off. Ronnie was ready to open the Range Rover's door for me but I hadn't had my quiet word with Bea Payne. I found her back in her office. Colin Weir, who had sensibly stayed out of a row which was none of his business, was occupying the other desk. There was something indefinably different about the room, more full of paper but undoubtedly more orderly. If a room could look relieved, this was doing so. The atmosphere was one of satisfaction.

'I thought we were never going to be rid of him,' Bea Payne said huskily. 'I can't thank you enough.'

'There may be others,' I said, 'though I hope not. If there are, call me. Now, how have you got on today?'

They beamed happily.

'We've done some good business,' Colin said. 'There were one or two new customers and we followed up a lot of earlier enquiries which seemed to have been left adrift.'

'At least Mr Maurice kept a list of approaches,' Bea said.

'Even if he didn't do anything about them,' Colin said. 'So far, seven farmers have agreed to demonstrations of major machinery.'

'I looked at the books and it's been the best day this year,' Bea said. 'By far.'

This was excellent news but I was not going to take it at face value. 'And who,' I asked, 'is going to demonstrate the machinery?'

'I am,' said Colin. He seemed surprised to have been asked the question. 'Miss Payne has heard most of the answers by now, but she can reach me on my mobile if anything tricky turns up.'

Things were working out better than I had ever hoped. 'That's very good. I think Mr Cowieson Senior believed in the philosophy that if you can build a better tractor the world will beat a path to your door,' I said, 'which may with reservations be true. But once the world has arrived at your door, you have to be both helpful and knowledgeable.'

'That's us,' Bea said cheerfully. 'I'm helpful and he's knowledgeable.'

'On that happy note,' I said, 'I'll leave you to get on with it.'

Chapter Six

That evening, the atmosphere at Hay Lodge had deteriorated. Elizabeth clearly felt both guilty and vulnerable. I was given to understand that she had been toying with the Internet messages, but from her listless and depressed attitude I could guess that any attempt to follow the electronic trail had been made in the shallow manner of one who knows that the task set is impossible. Duncan's degree had been in electronics and computing but Elizabeth's, I recalled, had been in mathematics, in which computers were merely tools of the trade, to be used rather than comprehended.

'The police should be able to sort this out in minutes,' she said angrily. 'Every time I think I'm making a little progress I come up against some obstructive bastard at Telecom or the Internet. I can*not* follow it up from the electronics alone and that's an end to the matter. We'd be better spending our energies harassing the Serious Fraud Office.'

Every attempt at encouragement from me or at technical assistance from her husband was deemed to be patronizing or was taken as criticism and she made no secret of her resentment. We dined in almost total silence and the wine decanter remained untouched.

When Elizabeth was in one of her (happily rare)

moods, there was little to be done but to stay clear. Duncan made a patently transparent excuse to go back to the shop for the evening, to finish off some urgent reprogramming which he had earlier admitted could have waited a week. I had no wish to spend the evening with Elizabeth who, hating herself, was taking her hatred out on anyone handy, but manners prevented me from taking too obviously to flight. For once, however, I was grateful for one of the phone calls which would normally have infuriated me. I answered the extension phone in the sitting room for no better reason than that Elizabeth, in the study and back at the computer, obviously had no intention of doing so. A not unattractive female voice assured me that she was not going to sell me anything – I could have assured her of that! – and then proceeded to extol the virtues of somebody's double glazing and conservatories.

I made vaguely affirmative noises and then hung up in the middle of the lady's peroration. I crossed the hall and put my head in at the study door. Elizabeth, with the main instrument at her elbow, was staring helplessly at a screen full of apparently unrelated letters and numerals. There was no indication that she had listened to my phone call.

'That was an old friend on the phone,' I said. 'I haven't seen him for years. You won't mind if I go and meet him at the hotel?'

Elizabeth who, for all her faults, was both well mannered and hospitable, would normally have suggested that I invite my friend to the house, but she seemed pleased at the prospect of having the place to herself. 'Go and have fun,' she said and heaved a sigh expressive of lonely martyrdom. Fun, it said, was for others to enjoy.

Once in the car, I reviewed my options. I had made several friends in the locality but there was always the possibility that Elizabeth might phone the hotel to speak to me, either to apologize for her curtness or more probably to seek advice about some estate problem which had arisen without warning. I nearly went back into the house to give her the number of my mobile, but she would have seen through that in seconds. So I descended the long hill, parked in the Square and entered through the hotel's plate-glass doors.

Much of the hotel's ground floor was taken up by the dining room with kitchen premises, a rambling public bar which was usually filled with voices raised above the sound of a jukebox and a large and suffocatingly formal lounge where the local dowagers sipped sherry or drank coffee according to the time of day. Fussier and more knowledgeable patrons, however, gravitated to a smaller and quieter cocktail bar tucked away off a minor lobby.

This, I found, was in its usual state of tranquillity. I exchanged a smile with the plump barmaid, a long-standing acquaintance – she being the wife, I hasten to add, of Ralph Enterkin. Two or three couples were whispering together in the darker corners, a salesman was studying his catalogues and the inside of a brandy snifter at an end of the bar while, at a table strategically placed between the bar and the hatch to the kitchen, Keith Calder was established with his wife and daughter. To judge from the debris on the table, they had taken a bar meal and Keith at least had enjoyed several whiskies. The residues in the ladies' glasses might have been tonic water or heeltaps remaining from large vodkas.

Keith beckoned to me and got up to appropriate another chair. 'You'll take a dram?' he asked.

'I'm not sure that I should,' I said. 'I had wine at lunchtime, followed by a brandy. It might not take much to put me back over the legal limit and I'm parked in full view of the police building.'

He smiled and his lived-in face became boyish again. 'I have two non-drinking drivers with me,' he said, 'and I'm sure that one of them can chauffeur you home.'

'In that case,' I said, 'and if the ladies won't mind, a dram would slip down well. Water please, no ice.'

Keith nodded and went to the bar. I turned to Deborah. 'I suppose Ian's too busy for socializing?' I suggested.

'He's busy,' she said. 'Baby-sitting. But he brought a whole stack of files home with him. I hope he isn't getting too lost to the world to hear a baby cry.' She frowned. 'Perhaps I'd better phone.'

'You'll do no such thing,' her mother said fondly. 'Ian dotes on that child. Anyway, little Bruce would hear the phone before Ian did. One hiccup and Ian's work will be forgotten.'

Deborah relaxed slowly.

Keith returned from the bar bearing a tray with two whiskies and two tonic waters. Mine I identified as Glenfiddich of no little age and at least a double. He raised his glass in brief salute.

'Here's hoping that all goes well,' he said carefully.

'I'll drink to that,' I said. I left it at that. Keith and his ladies, I knew, could be very discreet; but his intense curiosity had sometimes led him into investigations which in turn had led to a great deal of publicity.

Keith looked slightly put out but Molly hid a smile and leaned forward. 'Keith and Deborah told me about Saturday evening,' she said. 'They were quite sure that

Elizabeth had been caught out by the e-mail fraud. Deborah said that she looked ready to faint.'

I glanced around, keeping it casual, but the other drinkers were paying us no attention and the classical guitar music which was playing softly over hidden loud-speakers would have baffled a would-be eavesdropper. 'You haven't mentioned this to anyone else?' I asked.

She shook her head. 'Keith insisted that that kind of financial information needs to be kept under wraps. I take it that it was a lot of money?'

'From my humble viewpoint, a great deal of money. And – in the strictest possible confidence?'

They nodded and I knew that they would consider the agreement binding.

'It was already earmarked for the expansion at Agrotechnics,' I said. 'I've been rushing around drumming up alternative finance. I gather that we have little chance of seeing any of the original sum again.'

'And on top of your other worries,' Keith said, 'you go and stumble on Maurice Cowieson's body.'

The morning papers had reported the death but I had been relieved to see that they had made no mention as to who had found the body. I glanced at his daughter but she shook her head. 'I didn't tell him,' she said. 'I don't know how he always seems to know all about everything.'

'Word goes round,' Keith said, 'and I know a lot of people. I gather that Ian isn't convinced it was an accident.'

Deborah drew herself up and regarded her father disapprovingly. 'Now, that,' she said, 'I *definitely* didn't tell him because I didn't even know it myself.'

'Keep your voice down,' Keith said. He shrugged. 'I took a couple of ferrets onto Radburn Farm on Sunday, at the request of Johnny Duncan – the farmer,' he added in my direction. 'Johnny must have told Ian that I'd been there, because Ian arrived at the shop this morning to ask whether I'd seen anyone walking down the hill, across country.'

'And had you?'

'Not a soul,' Keith said regretfully. 'And Johnny hadn't either, because I asked him. Not that that means much, because there's a sunken path alongside the Den Burn which is totally screened by trees and hedges. But I hadn't heard of any other incidents and the only explanation for Ian's questions which occurred to me – after he'd left, unfortunately – was that somebody who drove a car up to the top might have walked back. And that strongly suggested to me that Ian thinks somebody drove Maurice's car to where you found it and walked back to the town. If he's right, that means that somebody was working alone.'

'Or that his accomplice was busy elsewhere or couldn't get hold of another car,' Molly said placidly.

Keith waved an airy hand. 'Or that,' he said. 'The really interesting question is this. What does Ian think happened? And why does he think it?'

'You really can't expect me to tell you that,' Deborah said.

'Because you don't know,' said her father. 'But Henry knows.'

The whiskies seemed to be finished so I got up for replenishments. Keith was pleased to accept another Glenfiddich but his wife and daughter declined. Mrs Enterkin did the necessary, took the money and came over to collect the empties. The interval gave me time for thought.

When we were alone again, I said, 'From what Ian told me, he probably thinks that somebody drove Cowieson's car up the hill and did get picked up by an accomplice. I don't know all of his reasons. I don't agree – I think I'd have heard another car. And that's all I'm saying. You can't expect me to tell you what Ian won't even tell his wife.'

'Another car could have freewheeled down the hill. There's one way to resolve this impasse,' Keith said. He took his mobile phone from an inside pocket and keyed in a number from memory. The call was answered immediately. 'Ian?' he said. 'Keith here. We've been joined by Henry Kitts. Deborah is pretending to know nothing about the death of Maurice Cowieson.' There was a pause. 'Well, maybe she does and maybe she doesn't, but have you any objection to us discussing it?' The phone made a faint squawking noise. Keith winked at me. 'Not in public and only in your presence? Just as you like. We'll be with you in about ten minutes.'

He switched the phone off and dropped it back into his pocket.

'You can't *do* that,' Deborah objected.

'Why not?'

'He's busy. And you haven't been invited.'

Keith's eyebrows shot up. 'I have now. And since when do I need a prior invitation to pay an informal call on my son-in-law?' He got to his feet. 'Are you coming? Or do I drive myself?'

'I have the car keys,' Molly said, producing and jingling them.

In answer, Keith produced a duplicate set, tossed them up and caught them, nearly fumbling the gesture. I was, and I remain, convinced that he was bluffing; but the threat was enough to get the party moving. When I stood up, I found that two double whiskies on top of whatever remained from my lunchtime wine and the later brandy had had an unsteadying effect. I was happy to hand my keys over to Deborah and to be shepherded tenderly into the front seat of the Calders' car. Keith settled in the back. Molly drove and she left us in no doubt that for two pins Keith would have been left to run behind. Molly's manner to her husband had always been an intriguing mixture of blind adoration with the attitude of a mother towards her idiot child. It would have been hard to say which predominated.

Deborah and her husband lived in a modest bungalow in a pretty street of recently built houses on the fringe of the town. Their red-tiled roof was within sight of the Hay Lodge windows, more than a mile away and a hundred-odd feet higher. Ian was scanning reports but he had anticipated our arrival by opening the front door, setting drinks beside his papers on the dining table which occupied one end of the lounge and putting a match to a log fire – which was for cosmetic effect only, being made superfluous by the central heating. When we came in he pushed aside his work, greeted us without any great sign of pleasure and started pouring. His whisky was good but not in the same class as the hotel's malt.

He looked first at his wife who, after planting a quick kiss on his left ear, had perched in her private little tapestry chair. 'All quiet,' he said, 'except for the occasional snore. We can switch this gadget off now. We don't want to broadcast our every word to the neighbours.' He turned off the child alarm while switching his eyes to Keith, who had settled in a dining chair opposite him. 'You'd better tell me what you're on about,' he said.

Keith took a sip of his whisky and managed not to show his disappointment in the blend. 'What I'm on about is that it's perfectly obvious you think that there's something not right about Maurice Cowieson's death and I'm damn sure that Deborah and Henry both ken fine what it's about and they won't say a word in case you skelp their backsides for gossiping about police business.'

Ian gave his father-in-law a look so reproachful that I would have thought them at daggers drawn if I had not known that they were habitually as thick as thieves. Ian, in his more relaxed moments, would sometimes admit that he might not have made his present rank and prospects without the several notable successes which he owed to Keith's help. But he had a point to make. 'And quite right too,' he said firmly. 'When folk with partial knowledge get to blethering it's never long before rumours begin to fly. When those rumours are wrong they're usually hurtful to somebody, but when they're right they can be seriously damaging. Leave the police to get on with their jobs and read about the results in your morning paper.'

'But,' said Keith helpfully.

Ian sighed and then laughed. 'But, in this one instance, I was going to ask for your help anyway. Tell me, all of you, what you know of the late Maurice Cowieson.'

Keith sneered at him – there's no other word for it. 'Come back down to earth,' he said. 'If you want us to help you, we need the facts. Or, anyway, we insist on having them. Why are you so sure that his accident wasn't accidental?'

Ian looked at me. 'You didn't tell them?'

'Not a word.'

'It's a pity that we didn't breed from you while we

had the chance. All right,' Ian told his father-in-law. He threw down the pencil which had seemed to be holding most of his concentration and looked up at the ceiling. 'This is not for general discussion yet, but I was going to take you into my confidence anyway. Mr Cowieson's car went straight over the brink without any attempt being made to brake or swerve. So, he could have had a heart attack or a fainting fit. But the fatal blow to his forehead was not in a position or at an angle that I could explain to myself. The driver's seat belt was fastened and his air bag had inflated, which should have prevented him from hitting the front pillar, but if he had managed to hit his head before the air bag restrained him I would have expected a more or less vertical blow on the right-hand side, high on the forehead; not a diagonal wound up at the hairline. There was also remarkably little blood spilled. Either he'd been given the whack on the head after he had passed on or, as Mr Kitts has suggested, somebody had washed his face because blood had had time to run in the wrong direction.

'The body had been pulled around and carried about so that it was very difficult to draw any conclusions from his clothing, but what I eventually saw was, let's say, not incompatible with his having been manhandled into the car and then across into the driver's seat after death.'

'He couldn't have been killed in the driver's seat?' Keith asked.

'I can't imagine any way in which the wound could have been in that place and at that angle. There wouldn't have been room for somebody inside the car with him to swing a weapon with such force and if he was hit through the window from outside the car the wound would certainly have slanted the other way.

124

'I've been jollying along my superiors in Edinburgh, reporting that the death appeared to be the result of an unfortunate accident but that I was investigating just in case there had been foul play.'

'I bet they've heard that from you before,' Keith said.

'It still works,' Ian assured him, 'because it suits their book as well as mine.' He tapped one of the folders on the table. 'But now I have the pathologist's report and so will they by tomorrow morning.'

Keith leaned forward. 'And it says . . .?'

'Pretty much what I've just told you about the wound, though in more scientific language. You won't be interested in ingrowing toenails and warts. He says that whatever broke the skull was straight, which rules out the faint possibility that he might have hit his head on the steering wheel; and round in cross-section, which eliminates the door pillar. There was neither blood nor hair on the door pillar, by the way. And it was that single blow to the head that killed him. It fractured and crushed his skull which, according to the pathologist, was of normal thickness.

'There was no drug or poison, no other wound and no sign of sudden illness. It's his opinion that death had already occurred before the crash but not very long before – there had been no time for hypostasis to develop and indicate any position other than seated in a car seat. The inevitable conclusion has to be foul play, almost certainly murder, which means that somebody more senior will come here, delighted to get out of Auld Reekie for a few days, and he'll bring his own team and expect my boys to wait on them hand and foot and he'll want to know why I haven't done all the things which will be obvious in the blinding light of hindsight,' Ian said hotly. 'So what

I want is to tie the damn thing up before he gets here and upsets everybody.'

'By tomorrow morning?' I said. 'You'll be lucky!'

'He won't be here tomorrow morning,' Ian said. 'When there's a local man and local manpower making a start on the donkey work, they never hurry themselves. He'll be issuing orders to me over the phone, while tidying his desk and using his team to clear away the details of previous cases. In a day or so, when the case is either solved or the tiresome part of the work has been sorted out, he'll arrive, ready to hold press conferences, claim the credit or pass on the blame.'

'They aren't all like that,' Keith said mildly. I was surprised to hear him coming to the defence of the police. I had heard him arguing the opposite. He and Ian, it seemed, had changed viewpoints.

'Not all,' Ian conceded. 'Just the eager beavers who get sent out into the sticks to show the yokels how it's done. But sometimes local knowledge is worth more than sophistication allied to manpower, and you have even more of that than I have. Now are you going to tell me about Maurice Cowieson? Or don't you know anything?'

We looked at each other, wondering who would open the bowling. The suggestion that he might be deficient in local knowledge stung Keith into speech. 'I never saw much of Maurice during our youth,' he said, 'because his father sent him away for an expensive education. Maurice wasn't very bright. As always happens, the combination of a sluggish mind educated above its capability was that he had an exaggerated idea of his own competence. He made enemies without even being aware of it.'

'Enemies?' Ian queried sharply.

Keith paused and then shrugged. 'Perhaps that's an

exaggeration. Let's just say that he put folks' backs up. He blundered through life, carried along by the money and the business his father had left him, and when he made mistakes he was too thick to recognize them and too proud to back down. He was quite sure that he was everybody's friend and that everyone loved him. And, of course, because he was so sure of it, some people did.'

'But not everybody?'

'Not by a mile. A thousand miles. A million light years.'

Molly's sympathy, always readily available, had been aroused. 'Whoever they send may not be as bad as you think,' she told Ian. 'We've met some very sympathetic ones. Or you may have solved it before he gets here.' (Ian looked even gloomier.) 'So we'd better help you while we can.' She paused, half frowning. She hated to say anything unpleasant about anyone but seemed to be having difficulty in the case of Maurice Cowieson. 'I don't remember meeting him often,' she said at last, 'maybe just a few times in passing, but when we were young he went around with more than one of my friends – at the same time, on occasions, because he was an awful man for the women. He married Edna James – remember her, Keith? – and he led her a dance. She had the boy within a year of their marriage and then she fell pregnant again and it killed her.' Molly paused again and then decided that it had to be told. 'Folks said that she gave up her hold on life, glad to be out of it.'

'I do remember Edna,' Keith said. 'She was no beauty but she was a good-hearted soul as well as being an only daughter in a well-to-do family. Maurice's father was a seedsman in a good way of business and Edna's father had a garage and engineering shop. The two businesses complemented each other and, under the old men, grew into the present business of agricultural supplies. Edna had a brother in farming who had the knack of spelling out just what service the farming world would be crying out for in a year's time, but he rolled a tractor over onto himself and died. Maurice had nothing to do but inherit. Then he set about ruining the business and Wallace said that he was sinking in the financial mire.' (Wallace is Keith's partner and man of finance.)

There was a pause while Keith refilled his glass and chose his words. 'He wasn't a man I'd care to mix with and he didn't shoot, so we rarely met and when his name was mentioned it was usually in connection with his chasing after the women – not always with much success, from what I heard.' There was, I thought, a tiny trace of amused superiority in Keith's voice. By reputation, he had been a devil for the women in his youth. Molly must have recognized the same tone, because I saw her throw him a tolerant glance that spoke volumes about the relationship which they had achieved and her confidence in the bond between them.

'Now that,' said Ian, 'could be very interesting. My sources mentioned some such interest but I gathered that those years were behind him now.'

'Your sources,' Deborah said, 'were trying to spare your blushes, or those of his lady-friends. He even tried it on with me when I went to ask him about a new lawnmower. He put his hand up my skirt – the white one with the pleats,' she added in her mother's direction.

Ian put his glass down with a thump and straightened his back. Suddenly he looked like thunder. 'You never told me that,' he snorted.

'No, of course I didn't,' Deborah said blithely. 'You'd

only have got all upset and probably done something silly. There was no need. Some men do that sort of thing and some don't. The time for you to get uptight about it would have been if I'd let him get away with it. I told him that he was a wicked old goat and he could bugger off. I also told him what to do with his lawnmower. We met again in the newsagent's a week later and he spoke as if nothing had ever happened, asking after you and saying wasn't the weather awful, which it was. He seemed to take acceptance or rejection as a normal part of life and nothing for either side to get upset about.'

Ian took a thoughtful pull at his whisky. 'Somehow I've lost my motivation to solve this case,' he said. 'Anybody who cared to kill Maurice Cowieson can't be all bad. And you didn't hear me say that.'

'Of course not,' said his wife. 'I know when you're only joking – you were only joking, weren't you? I'll tell you something else. At the shoot dinner, while Henry was talking to Mrs Ombleby, somebody said that Miles's father wouldn't be pleased as he was setting his cap at her. It may just have been malicious gossip—'

'I'd heard that in the town,' said Molly, 'so there may be something in it. She owns half of Edinburgh, so that may have been the attraction. She could easily have bailed him out of his money troubles. She's not very attractive in any other way.'

'Oh, I don't know,' said her husband reflectively. 'She's amusing company, which can't always be said about rich widows, and I suspect that she may be one of those apparently passionless women who suddenly catch fire. I've been told about them,' he added quickly. 'What's more difficult to understand is what the women ever saw in him.'

'That's not so difficult,' Molly said. 'He had a good line in chat. He could make little jokes that had double meanings hidden in them, but never going over the line and beyond the point that would be sort of appropriate to the stage he'd reached with whoever he was talking to. The stage of intimacy – you know what I mean?' she asked anxiously. We reassured her. 'And he had old-fashioned good manners – courtly, sort of – and he was always very neat and clean. It could have worked, him and Mrs Ombleby. There are worse reasons for marriage than financial interest.' She was still in the throes of a long-standing and happy marriage, so that she would have liked to see the rest of the world tidily coupled.

Keith looked at her. Molly had a *Mona Lisa* smile. After a hesitation, Keith resumed. 'The only other whisper was that when he went to the bank to make a deposit they had to prise his fingers apart before he could bear to let go.'

'That I could well believe,' I said.

'Ah, yes.' Ian leaned back in his chair and looked at me expectantly. 'I was going to come to you about his business affairs.'

'And I was going to come and tell you about them,' I said. I looked around. 'Still in confidence?' I received a succession of nods which I knew would be honoured. 'Cowieson's upbringing, from what's been said, was typical, guaranteed to produce exactly what it did – a well educated, highly trained nincompoop. He had his contract to retail Agrotechnics's agricultural machinery long before I was appointed to the board or I would have fought tooth and nail to see it awarded to somebody else, anybody else, even at worse terms. What he's managed to sell has sold because it's good stuff and people have tracked him down and pushed money at him.

'Until a few years ago, a farmer couldn't lose money if he tried. Some of that easy money rubbed off on his suppliers. Then things got tough. Now, with cattle and sheep in serious decline, a great deal of pasture is being turned over to arable, making a considerable demand for new machinery. Agrotechnics is booming but Cowieson wasn't attacking the new market. His methods were too old-fashioned to be believable. Word of mouth and handing out a few brochures. He grudged money spent on advertising. There was allowance in the costs for giving a handsome kickback to farmers but Maurice seems to have kept that for himself. God knows where it went. Any profit that the business made seems to have vanished.'

'Spent on his women,' Deborah said. 'You know how word goes round in a small community. From what I hear, he never grudged gifts of jewellery or Thai silk undies, provided there was going to be a return in you-know-what.'

'That could explain a great deal,' I said. 'As a result of plain bad management, aggravated by a comparatively minor fire, his sales fell short of the figure he was required by his contract to take from Agrotechnics – a figure which none of the other agencies had the least difficulty in meeting. Result – overstocking and a huge debt to the manufacturer, but he still refused to give up the agency. He seems to have had a remarkable talent for deluding himself. He could close his mind to anything he didn't want to think about and believe what he wanted to believe.

'The first thing I did when I became a director was to insist that he grant a floating charge, virtually putting

131

up his stock and business as security for the debt. We interviewed him last Friday and he swore that he was expecting a fresh injection of finance and would settle the debt. Maybe he was pinning his hopes on a quick courtship of the wealthy widow. But it would only have taken a more intensive selling campaign to put things right within a couple of years and if we'd seen an improvement in his methods we'd have given him more time. He couldn't see that. We were on the point of fore-closing on him and putting in a manager with a proven track record when . . . this happened.'

'Which would raise the spectre of suicide but for the pathologist's report,' Keith said. 'Men have driven off the road before now to escape from their worries. Perhaps she turned him down.'

Ian was frowning. He made another note. 'I'll have to try the pathologist again. Between us, we may have missed something.'

'His situation was worse even than I've told you so far,' I said reluctantly. The fact that I had disliked the builder made me perversely more reluctant to put him forward as a suspect. 'When somebody grants a floating charge, the company's documents at Register House are endorsed accordingly. While I was at Cowieson's this afternoon, Allardyce, the builder, turned up. He claimed to be under the impression that he too had been granted a floating charge. It was dated later than ours and ours had been properly arranged and registered by Agrotech-nics's solicitors. Allardyce admitted that he'd taken Cowieson's word for it that the floating charge had been properly registered.'

'Then how—?' Ian began. He stopped. '*Claimed to be?*

You think that Allardyce might have discovered earlier that he'd been sold a pup?'

'I leave thinking to you,' I said. 'I worded myself carefully, that's all. The way I read it is that Maurice Cowieson saw the floating charge as a splendid way of getting creditors off his back while he looked for alternative sources of finance.'

'An act of deliberate fraud?'

'That's how I see it, assuming that Mr Allardyce was telling the truth. It certainly isn't the kind of thing that can happen by mistake.' I paused while I considered my words. 'You'll have to see him yourself, of course. If you're looking for opinions, I think that the existence of a prior floating charge was news to Mr Allardyce, unless he's a superlative actor.'

'Which he isn't,' Deborah said. 'He's a member of the drama society but his acting was so wooden and unconvincing that we have him painting scenery and taking tickets and occasionally carrying a tray on stage. You've more need to look very hard at Miles Cowieson. If his father was playing silly beggars and throwing the business down the drain . . .'

'Did you think I'd forgotten him?' Ian enquired. 'At the moment, it seems clear that when his father died he was already in the air, on a plane to Amsterdam. It would have been just possible, but very unlikely, for a lookalike to have gone in his place, but nothing else has come up so far to support the possibility. I'm afraid that we have to count him out.' Ian gave a sigh which would have blown out the candles on a centenarian's birthday cake. He pushed the stack of reports away from him, got to his feet and came to replenish my glass. 'Without a lucky break, I'm not going to solve this one. There's so little to go on that I can only start from motives; and that's always a shaky start because crimes are often committed for motives that a sensible man would consider ridiculous. But murderers aren't sensible men.'

'What about your forensic boffins?' Keith said. 'What have they told you?'

'Very little,' Ian said. 'We aren't sure yet where he died.'

'But the car . . .?'

'Not much more. No unexpected fingerprints, just the smudges of gloved fingers. Plenty of hairs, mostly long and tinted, but if we trace all the women who've been in his car, what will that tell us?'

'It may furnish useful DNA corroboration when you find your murderer,' Keith pointed out.

'If, not when,' Ian said gloomily. 'And any woman could come up with quite a convincing reason for having been in that car.'

There was a gloomy silence. Molly was ready to contribute another ill-judged snippet of optimism. Before she could drive Ian the rest of the way up the wall, I jumped in. 'And you've no more news about the missing money?' I asked.

He shook his head, but at least the chance to spoil my day seemed to brighten his own outlook. 'Not a word,' he said more cheerfully. 'It's been referred to the Serious Fraud Office and it remains their baby until they've dealt with it.'

'And they will get round to that when?'

'God knows,' Ian said.

Chapter Seven

At my age, I had every right to be badly hung over after a vinous lunch and a sip of brandy followed by an evening during which, when I came to look back, rather a lot of whisky had been taken. But in the morning I had no more than a mild headache, a mere dull nagging in the brain, which was better than I deserved.

Our visit to Ian's and Deborah's house had continued for some time after the lady of the house had begun to hint that bed was calling. (Hospitality runs in the Calder family and, once Ian had appreciated the amount of background information being heaped on him, he produced a second bottle.) I had weakly accepted rather more of Ian's whisky than was wise. When Keith was almost ready to move, Deborah had driven me, in my own car, up the hill, followed by Molly in the other car to bring her back. Elizabeth and Duncan had already retired and the house was dark and silent. I crept to bed, careful not to stumble. I had no wish for an admonitory lecture. I suspected that Isobel had had a word in Elizabeth's ear, suggesting that she might steer me away from the indulgences to which old men are vulnerable. Whatever the reason, there was sometimes a tendency for my role and Elizabeth's to reverse.

A late breakfast, served by Joanna and taken in solitary state, soon put me more or less right and I found that my mind was back in gear. Duncan had already left for work but I found Elizabeth in the study, dealing in a lacklustre manner with the morning's mail.

She greeted me a little more cheerfully than before and I gathered that she had come to terms with her loss and at least partially forgiven herself for her folly. It was inevitable that she would hear about my evening with the Calders so I invented a few lies about my friend's early departure and gave her a foreshortened and edited version of my real evening.

I finished by asking whether she had made any progress with tracing the e-mail fraud. She shrugged and went rapidly through all the signs of one who has abandoned hope. 'I can't seem to find a starting point which wouldn't immediately come up against the need for a court order or whatever it is you need to make some bossy, petty-minded prat cough up some useful but relatively harmless information,' she said. 'And if the police and the Serious Fraud Office, with their access to bank and telephone records, haven't got anywhere . . .'

A kick-start was called for if she was to be boosted out of her lethargy and despond. My own understanding of the Internet was about as deep as my comprehension of the binomial theorem, but sometimes the ignorant eye will be caught by something which is too obvious for the expert to see. 'Do you have those two printouts handy?' I asked her.

Elizabeth sighed. 'While you're about it, you may as well go for a stroll across the loch,' she said tartly. But she handed me a folder from her desk. As I feared, apart from the addresses and the message the pages were taken up with gobbledegook. Try as I might, I could not recognize anything significant. If there was nothing helpful in the printing itself, perhaps there might be more value in the differences. I looked from the copy that Gordon had given me to the fraudulent one which had deceived Elizabeth, beginning, for lack of any reason to the contrary, with the topmost line. 'As I understand it,' I said, 'addresses and file references have to be correct, right down to the spaces and punctuation. Right?'

'Quite right,' she said with excessive patience. 'It would use up rather a lot of memory to program a computer to select the nearest approximation to the right address and, of course, it would hardly do for confidential mail to fetch up in the wrong hands.'

I ignored her patronizing manner. 'There's probably a simple explanation,' I said slowly, 'which I'm not wise enough to see, but these are slightly different.' I showed her the first message, which opened with FROM: INTERNET:CompuServe@Controller.net. The other began FROM:INTERNET:Compuserve@Controler.net. 'Are those just mistakes?' I asked her. 'Or is there any significance?'

She frowned, her interest gradually sharpening. 'If those were typographical errors,' she said, 'the message would still have arrived here.' I began to deflate. 'But,' she said, 'the address of origin is put in automatically by the sender's machine. And I clicked on REPLY at the bottom of the message. Any error there and he wouldn't have got my reply and we'd have been saved this whole horrible hoo-ha. I suppose it's possible that they built in a difference for sorting purposes, but I can't see any reason for it with two identical messages. Why didn't I notice the discrepancy?'

'Who really reads the address at the top of a letter

without a special reason?' I asked rhetorically. 'Same principle.'

She gave a sigh of relief and favoured me with a smile, almost her first since we had discovered the loss. 'God bless you, Uncle Henry! I was beginning to wonder if I'd totally lost my marbles, but that makes me feel a little saner. Do you see what it means?'

I put my finger on the earlier copy. 'I'm told that these have been turning up all over the world. My guess would be that somebody who received one decided to jump on the bandwagon. He – or she—' I added for the sake of political correctness, 'may even have fallen for it and wanted to recoup their loss.'

'Some recouping!' she said bitterly. 'Yes, that's exactly how I see it.'

'As you say. They would then have to have a similar but slightly different address. There would be no point in the exercise if useful information simply went back to the original fraudster. How would they have got your e-mail address?'

'Easily. Perhaps the easiest way of all would be to look at the correspondence in what they call the "forums". I've been using them a lot – they make a simple and easy way to get free advice from experts. Where do we go from here?'

I looked at her in surprise. My first thought was that she should be in a better position to answer that question. Then I realized that under the veneer of education she was still an unsophisticated girl and that I had far more experience in matters of financial chicanery. We were silent for several minutes while I thought it out. 'You'd better call Duncan home if, as you said, he's more familiar with the subtleties of programming,' I said.

'I will if you say so. But I don't think he'd be able to get far without the powers that the police can call on.'

'Maybe you're right,' I said. 'I've probably been given quite a false impression that the whole system's wide open by all the talk about "hacking in". The police can get access to banking and telephone records. We'll have to keep them informed anyway. We'd better get in touch with Ian Fellowes.'

She turned the phone round on the desk and read me out the number of the local station. Detective Inspector Fellowes, I was told, was in a meeting but would call me back. I disconnected. Remembering my own dictum that *nobody ever calls you back*, I decided to phone again every half-hour or so until I got Ian on the phone.

Within a few seconds, the phone rang. I made a mental apology to Ian, but the voice which came on the line was that of Mr Stoep. Could he come through this afternoon to inspect and value the available treasures? Rather than prolong the discussion and risk losing Ian's return call (if it ever came), while thinking that Ronnie could do the honours if I was otherwise engaged, I said that he would be welcome.

I was explaining Mr Stoep to Elizabeth when the phone rang again. This time it was Ian. 'Thank you,' I told him. 'You're very prompt.' I went on to explain how a further examination of the e-mails suggested that more than one fraudster was at work, using almost identical formats.

'That's the first suggestion of the kind,' Ian said. 'I'll pass it on to the Serious Fraud Office but it may not be enough to jump your case to the front of the queue.' His voice went from speculative to decisive. 'I'd better come up and see you. Would this evening suit?'

139

I consulted Elizabeth briefly. 'That would be perfect,' I said. 'But . . . are you sure you can get away?'

'The hotshot from Edinburgh has arrived, ahead of my prognostication.' There was a long pause. I guessed that Ian was making certain that he was not overheard. 'As I feared, he's being highly critical of all that's gone before. I'm in the process of handing over what I've got so far and he's not impressed. I think he's looking forward to reporting on my failures when he's brought the case to a triumphant conclusion. After I've given him the lot, I think he'll want me out of his hair. About eight?'

I agreed and we ended the call. 'He's coming at about eight,' I told Elizabeth. 'I leave it to you to decide whether to get Duncan home and go as far as you can before Ian gets here.'

'I don't think that there's anything he could do,' she said. 'On top of which, I made up my mind never to remind Duncan that I'm the one with the money. He refused to accept a marriage settlement, you may remember.'

'Then he has no right to be sensitive about it.'

'I'm trying to make sure that he never does become sensitive about it,' she said.

'Successfully?'

'He's better about it than I ever dared hope,' she said. Then she spoiled it by adding, 'So far,' in a thoughtful tone.

When Mr Stoep arrived it was in an enormous Volvo estate – chosen, I supposed, for its ability to carry small to medium-sized lots on behalf of less well equipped clients. When I considered that many of the clients selling valuables would be elderly widows, I could see the logic of his choice.

With Ronnie as guide and furniture-shifter, we started our tour in the house. Mr Stoep admired the John Emms foxhounds but pronounced my estimate out of date. He put its value at twice my figure. At ten thousand pounds it would make good almost one per cent of Elizabeth's loss. But, I reminded myself, the big is only the accumulation of a lot of littles or, in the Scots, mony a mickle maks a muckle. He put a disappointing figure on the miniatures.

We moved on to the outbuildings. From the first, disappointment was in the air. The previous house on the present site had burned to the ground many years earlier and very little of its contents had been saved. But the original family seat had been up north in an even more gloomy but otherwise similar baronial hall. When Peter's wife, Lady Hay, had no longer been around to cherish ostentation above comfort, he had been quick to dispose of it, complete with all sporting rights and such contents as the purchaser had had a fancy for. Some of the smaller and better of what Peter had been left with had been used to furnish the new house. The remainder had then been stored in the stables of the original building, which had escaped the fire, and in the attic of the new house. Those in the outbuildings seemed to consist of items too massive for most modern homes, not of particularly good periods and mostly infested with woodworm, furniture beetle, death-watch beetle and a variety of moulds and fungi – everything, as Mr Stoep said, but dandruff. One table which would otherwise have been of value had been transported at some time to India and embellished with carving by some local craftsman. Try as he might, Mr Stoep could not bring his estimate of the value at auction to a figure which would contribute noticeably to our present deficit. We earmarked half a dozen pieces for the saleroom, in the hope that some rich eccentric might have a rush of blood to the head on sale day.

We adjourned to the house and climbed to the spacious, floored and lined attic. Here, under the broad skylights and the electric lamps, the prospect was a little brighter. Mr Stoep searched through the pictures, mostly Victorian oil paintings by artists of whom I had never heard, of gloomy subjects made gloomier by their treatment and by the bitumen which was leaching out of the paints. He made use of such cheerless phrases as 'on a good day' and 'given a little competition between collectors', but his total estimate began to grow by thousands instead of hundreds. Much of the china was chipped and incomplete although an almost complete tea-and-dinner service for twenty-four people, by Wedgwood, dating from around 1800, made a useful but still far from sufficient contribution. An early Lowestoft dish from around 1760 and a Sèvres chamber pot would have made substantial contributions but for some bad cracks. An Edward Clifford watercolour had at some time hung in too bright a room and was badly faded.

I was losing heart and on the point of apologizing to Mr Stoep for wasting so much of his valuable time when we came to the last item, half hidden by an art deco screen of singular hideousness and a Turkish rug which turned out to be sadly worn and moth-eaten. This was a long, ornate Japanese box from, I guessed, the late seventeenth century.

'Fake?' I suggested from the depths of my disenchantment.

Mr Stoep studied the decoration through a lens. 'Not a bit of it,' he said. 'Perfectly genuine.'

'Made for export?'

He sighed. 'You would be so easy to rob blind,' he said. 'Sometimes I wish I was a crook. This was made for the house of a very rich man. Tell me, how much would you hope to get for it?'

His words implied a considerable value so I thought of a number and doubled it. 'Twenty K?' I suggested. I waited for his cry of derision.

'At that price I'd take three of them. And I haven't even looked inside yet. If it's what I think it is . . .'

He brushed away a layer of dust and lifted the lid. About twenty of what looked like glass slides in gold or gilt frames were slotted into place in a long row. He drew two of them out and handed one to me. I received it gingerly. It would be in line with our current luck if I should break one and spoil the set. The neat, gold frame held a thick glass plate embellished on each side with an exquisite painting, a landscape with figures, perhaps six inches square. The paintings were executed in lustrous enamel and the salient details were raised in tiny, ivory carvings.

'Now how much?' Stoep asked.

I tried to imagine one of the paintings suitably framed coming up for auction and visualized the bidding. Then I multiplied the figure by forty. The resultant sum was so far beyond credibility that I scaled it down. 'Fifty thou'?' I suggested.

He snorted with amusement. In his eye I could see the gleam of the true enthusiast on a hot trail. 'Even for what you can see, you're a long way on the mean side. Now let's have another look. I've seen one of these before. Not as good, not as big and not in such good condition but I think . . . say a little prayer . . .'

He studied the example in his hand and fiddled with the ornamentation of the frame. 'This hasn't been touched since Victoria was a girl,' he said. But he must have found the catch he was looking for, because something clicked and moved and I saw that the 'slide' was composed of two pieces of glass with a third sandwiched between. He drew out this third piece and held it very carefully for me to see. Again, each side was painted in glowing colours by a master hand, with the intimate little details raised in ivory, but this time the subject matter would have brought a blush to the cheek of . . . But no. Examples typifying sufficient breadth of mind are outside my experience. I can only say that I have never seen nor dared to imagine such lavishly erotic concepts. That these were intensely pleasurable to the participants, male and female, was more than evident from the expressions meticulously displayed on their faces. Even Ronnie was looking curious but mildly shocked.

Stoep looked up from the example in his hand. 'I doubt if Sir Peter ever knew that these were there,' he said. 'This is not the kind of thing that was discussed and handed round within families. It was probably brought back from the Orient by one of Sir Peter's ancestors, who would have enjoyed it in secret and then taken that secret to the grave with him. To his descendants, it would just be a box of rather pretty pictures.'

'I'm certain that Mrs Ilwand doesn't know,' I said. 'And I hope she never will. Just at the moment, after years of considering her late grandfather to be an outdated fuddy-duddy, she's come round to thinking of him as a sort of latter-day saint. I wouldn't want to sow any doubts in her mind.'

'I would have thought,' Mr Stoep said gently, 'that the fact that the box has been gathering dust in the attic should have been reassurance enough.'

'All the same, could you conduct a sale discreetly? We can credit the balance to the estate without being too specific about exactly what went under the hammer?'

'We can do that, though you may be worrying need-lessly. Women can be very matter-of-fact about pornography. Usually, they think it's rather funny.'

'Let's not chance it. Her grandmother would certainly have ordered that it be taken outside and smashed up. Ronnie?' I said.

'I'll haud my wheesht.' He sounded rather subdued.

'Your turn now,' I told Stoep. 'What value would you put on it now?'

He gave the glass pane a last, loving look and then gently slid it back into its slot and replaced both slides in the box. 'I wouldn't care to put a figure on it,' he said. 'For once, I'm at a loss. I can think of several collectors who would give all their teeth for it and probably throw in a testicle as a makeweight. Get them competing in a private auction by telephone and you're in write-your-own-cheque territory.' He produced his ever-present note-book and pen. 'I'll send a van for the other items some time next week, but I'm going to write you out a receipt for this one item and take it away with me now. It is simply too precious to remain here, now that we may have drawn attention to the possible existence of some-thing valuable.'

We made a very quick inspection of all the inner

slides – it had occurred to me that Mr Stoep or one of his minions might be tempted to make off with all but the two we had seen and swear that the others must have been sold or damaged many years ago. I made sure that the receipt recorded the fact that the set was complete and undamaged. 'How long before we can expect to see the money?' I asked.

'To realize its full value, we must make haste slowly. At a guess, some time early in the New Year.'

We left it at that. I had Ronnie carry the box down to Mr Stoep's car and I preceded him down the steep little stair just in case he tripped on the way down. I might still mend again, I felt, but all that glass would not.

An accident between Newton Lauder and Edinburgh would result in almost infinite complications. Before Mr Stoep left, I took him into the vacant sitting room and made him phone his insurers to arrange special cover. The value that he put on the Japanese box for insurance purposes almost put me into a state of shock but his insurers seemed to take it as a matter of course.

I watched him drive away, just to reassure myself that he was driving with appropriate care. I had a little bet with myself that before he was ten miles up the road he would pull in to the verge and have a private gloat over the hoard. I considered making it a condition of the sale that I should receive a set of photographs. But then I thought of Isobel's face if she came across them after my death and I put the idea out of my mind.

Elizabeth's inheritance seemed secure again. In my relief, I was walking six inches above the floor. All the same, when Elizabeth asked me at dinner how we had got on I only said that things looked hopeful. In part, this was because Joanna was in the room, serving the main course; but also because, in the antiques business, the old proverb about cups and lips applies many times over. A second opinion might pronounce the cabinet a fake. Or the Hay family title to it might be disputed. Or a scandal in the media might result in no one bidding for it. I had no wish to see Elizabeth indulging in extravagant investments on the basis of a windfall which might never arrive.

'The signs,' I said when Joanna had left, 'are that you can meet your obligations and that we may not have to borrow from our lottery winner for as long as I feared.'

'But I have to tell Mrs Ombleby not to count on my backing?'

Rather than risk seeing Elizabeth lose the chance of a profitable investment because of my caution, I had to follow a compromise course. 'Stay in touch with her. You never know.' I decided to borrow a couple of phrases from Mr Stoep. 'On a good day, and given a little competition between collectors, anything can happen.'

Elizabeth nodded. 'I'll send her an e-mail, holding out hope.'

That caught my attention. 'You've been exchanging e-mails with her? Is she – what do they call it? – computer-literate?'

'Very,' Elizabeth said, laughing. 'She used to teach computing at one of the technical colleges. Just now she's working full time on the computer programs for the new business. They have to gather up all the best recipes and allow for people who don't like this or that, for visitors at one meal but not the others that day, and they have to make allowances for vegetarians and diabetics and vegans. And it all needs to be digitized, so that somebody

147

can look in the menu catalogue and phone or e-mail some simple codes. Keeping it simple can get very complicated.'

I could see what she meant. I was on the verge of pointing out that Mrs Ombleby would seem to be one person who knew the e-mail address and was trying to raise huge sums of money, but Elizabeth's next words distracted me. 'One of those paintings was believed to be by Raeburn,' she said. 'Isn't that right?' she added to Duncan.

'Don't bring me into it,' Duncan said placidly. 'It's your money and your heirlooms. I only know what you've told me.'

'School of,' I told Elizabeth. 'And not a very apt pupil.' Then I realized that a reputed Raeburn might make a satisfying explanation for an unexpectedly large windfall. I took comfort from the fact that the sale of a collection of antique Japanese pornography was unlikely to be the subject of a press release. I preferred her never to know that her grandfather, whether he knew it or not, had bequeathed to her about forty pieces of top quality erotic art. 'But that's only my opinion,' I added hastily. 'We'll have to see what the experts make of it. I think you'll be able to go ahead with your warning reflectors.'

'Now?' she asked quickly.

'Not yet,' I said cautiously. 'I don't think you could get it done in time for most of this season's long hours of darkness anyway. Did you make any progress tracing the e-mails?'

She looked smug. 'A little. The e-mail to me definitely originated in Britain. Code one nine four is the UK. And they used the service provider Demon. I couldn't make head nor tail of anything else. I thought we'd wait until we'd seen Ian.'

148

'We've already waited about four days,' I said. 'I don't suppose another will matter. We'll see Ian together. Then, when you can escape, try to leave me alone with him and I'll see what else I can find out.'

Elizabeth's mood had improved markedly, perhaps in celebration of her modest success. Her manner became flirtatious and Duncan, seeing the resumption of marital relations as a very real prospect, responded. My own mood, following Mr Stoep's discovery, was already upbeat. We had another glass of wine apiece and exchanged mildly *risqué* stories.

Ian brought the jollity to an end by arriving as we finished our meal. He brought with him an untidily dressed young woman with a dumpy figure and rather coarse features who yet managed to exude sex appeal. This puzzled me at first until I pinned it down as being the outcome of full lips, perfect skin and eyelids which drooped over large and lustrous eyes. This appeal was not just my uncertain opinion but was visibly echoed by Duncan and I saw Elizabeth's hackles rise. Ian introduced her as WDC McLure. Deborah had already fed them both, Ian explained, declining the offer of coffee on their joint behalves.

We settled in the study.

'I brought Miss McLure along because she has relevant expertise,' Ian said. 'She has a computing degree from Strathclyde and we met on the course on computer fraud. She's been in on several computer fraud cases including a major embezzlement.'

Miss McLure looked modest.

'Glad to have you along,' I told her. She smiled faintly but remained silent.

'It's a stroke of luck that I could borrow her from

149

Edinburgh,' Ian said. 'She was free and she came straight away. I've told her the background in strictest confidence. So . . . what fresh news do you have for us?'

Elizabeth and Duncan looked at me. I found it strange that they should defer to me in an area where their expertise was so much greater than mine. Apparently the honour was mine because I had noticed the first discrepancy. 'Nothing seemed to be happening,' I said, 'so I had a good look at two versions of the e-mail, the one that was sent to Mrs Ilwand and another which I had been given in Edinburgh. I took a close look at the addresses. These are usually taken on trust, which I suppose is why nobody seems to have noticed two differences. One of the few things I know about e-mail addresses is that you have to get every letter, every punctuation mark and any spaces right or the computers don't recognize it. But take a look for yourselves. There's a spelling mistake and the omission of a capital letter. Perhaps there's some other explanation, but I suspect that somebody was duplicating the original fraud and made inconspicuous changes to the address in order to route the replies back to himself. Then Mrs Ilwand took a good look at the rest of the gobbledegook following the address and discovered that hers originated in Britain whereas we understood that the main series comes from Canada. What we want to know is, do we wait for it to come to the front of the SFO queue, do we call it to their attention now in the hope that they'll give it priority or do we look into it ourselves?'

Ian and WDC McLure pored over the two papers. 'My guess would be the same as yours,' Miss McLure said suddenly. It was immediately obvious why she was sparing in her use of words. Her voice was musical but her accent was atrocious, stemming from Glasgow at its discordant worst. At least, I decided, she was not trying to hide it under that veneer of gentility which is so much more demeaning than the natural voice. 'The one to Mrs Ilwand did come from a different source, originating in the UK. And the other one is Canadian. That, of itself, isn't conclusive, of course. Anyone could have sent any of them from anywhere. It's even possible to route messages through somebody else's mainframe. But the indications of a different point of origin are certainly there.'

Elizabeth, on the introduction into her home of another young woman, and one gifted with more insidious sex appeal than herself, had been looking distinctly put out, but now she brightened again. I thought that the feet of clay – in the form of the atrocious accent – might have had a lot to do with it. 'That's what I thought,' Elizabeth said. 'And it came through Demon, another service provider. I called Demon, but they couldn't or wouldn't tell me anything about the source.'

'We can find out where it came from,' said the WDC. 'We can probably find what identity he gave himself. Not that that'll get us very far on its own. There are too many ways to break the trail, but I dare say we can get there eventually.' She looked at her cheap, digital watch. 'But not tonight. The banking day ends at five and the out-of-hours staff at the service providers can't find their own bums in the dark to scratch them. I'll make a start in the morning. Don't expect miracles.'

'You'll keep us posted?' I asked anxiously. When Ian hesitated, I went on, 'I know that it's against your principles to tell the victims anything. The law gives the criminal, the police and the courts all kinds of rights but the victim is considered to be nothing but a bloody nuisance who should have had more sense than to be mugged, defrauded, assaulted or otherwise abused in the first place.'

Duncan looked shocked, Elizabeth less so, but Ian grinned. 'You've been listening to my father-in-law,' he said.

'My opinions are my own,' I told him, though in fact I knew that the extra glass of wine was doing the talking.

'I don't go all the way with you, but I agree that the accused should have less rights and, yes, the victim should have more.'

I gave him back his grin. 'That's very handsome,' I said. 'But in this instance it will cost Sir Peter's estate even more money if we can't make the right decisions; and we can't make them if we don't know what's coming next and approximately when.'

Ian sighed. 'You have a cynical but generally accurate view. In fact, you still sound very much like my revered father-in-law. In this instance, however, you can see for yourselves, probably better than I can, that any leakage of information about the fraud and our progress towards solving it could affect the market and damage your credit. Because it might cost you more of the money that you were so anxious about, I think I can trust you to treat the information as confidential. In any case, we'll have to refer to you for information. So I'll see that you're kept informed.'

The discussion seemed to be drawing to a close. Elizabeth suddenly remembered the obligations of a hostess. 'Where is Miss McLure going to sleep?' she asked. 'We have several bedrooms spare here.'

'That's very helpful of you,' the WDC said. 'But I'll go back to Edinburgh.'

'Miss McLure thinks nothing of long drives,' Ian said, 'and she seems to get by on an absolute minimum of sleep. I'm told that she's a chronic insomniac. She'll be at work sharp in the morning.'

Miss McLure ignored the statement as if it was too obvious to have been worth stating.

Elizabeth and Duncan began to get up. I sat tight. But Ian surprised us. 'We'd like a word with Mrs Ilwand,' he said. 'And later with her husband.'

'What about?' Duncan asked sharply.

Ian made a vague gesture. 'We were coming up here anyway, so Detective Chief Inspector Dornoch – the officer investigating the death of Mr Cowieson – has asked me to clear up a few points. Miss McLure is not strictly on that inquiry but I'd prefer her to remain.' Ian's manner had darkened now that we were back to the topic of the murder. He was no longer rendering official assistance to social acquaintances. I guessed that the incoming Detective Chief Inspector's remarks were rankling and that Ian suspected his present errand of having been created to furnish another opportunity to blacken him with higher authority.

Duncan nodded reluctantly and got up to leave the room. It seemed to me that the police suspected a connection between the fraud and the murder although, on what little we knew so far, coincidence might well have been at work. Police are suspicious of coincidences but in my experience so many things are happening at any given moment that many of them will inevitably coincide. 'Perhaps Mrs Ilwand would like me to be present,' I suggested. I noticed that WDC McLure was inconspicuously taking shorthand.

Ian looked surprised but not concerned. 'If she

wishes,' he said. 'After all, she remains your ward for another few months.'

But Elizabeth treated me to one of her rare smiles. 'Thanks, Uncle Henry,' she said. 'It's very thoughtful of you but I really must learn to . . . to stand on my own feet.' I guessed that she had only just restrained herself from saying 'wipe my own bottom', an expression which she had taken to using whenever we discussed her assumption of responsibilities.

I got up. 'I'm sure you've got nothing to worry about,' I said. I followed Duncan into the sitting room but only for a minute or so. I was feeling uncertain and perhaps a little guilty, because I had intended to point Ian in the direction of several people who might well have had motivation towards one crime or the other. A minority of people rush to the police to accuse each other of criminal behaviour but most of us have a hang-up about it. For many, it may be the fear of reprisals; but I trace my own reluctance to my schooldays when peer loyalty made it unthinkable that one should 'sneak' or, in Scotland, 'clype'.

There remained a few of Peter Hay's cigars, still safely shrouded in their individual metal condoms and quite smokeable. I fetched one from the humidor and carried it out with me onto the lawn.

A good cigar is not to be hurried, particularly if it is being enjoyed in the afterglow of several glasses of excellent wine. I paced gently to and fro, enjoying the sounds of the night. The weather had cleared and it was a mild autumn night without a trace of dew. A bright moon was washing colour out of the garden. The silver birches shone brightly against a universally black background. An owl swept silently overhead. Newton Lauder was a sprinkle of lights down in the valley and a faint mutter of distant traffic. Spin, the spaniel, came out of the shadows and joined me but, sensing my mood, remained quietly and companionably at heel. He seemed to be deep in thoughts of his own but he was probably only waiting for something to happen.

I had intended to clear my mind of all thoughts of money and greed, of crime and violence, but soon I found that it had entered a mood of wild speculation. Neither Elizabeth nor Duncan was capable of murder; of that I was sure, but in any event I had left Elizabeth in the house while surely the murder had been in progress. And she could have had no motive, beyond a minor tax advantage, for embezzling her own money.

But Duncan had gone off in his six-year-old Cavalier nearly an hour before the fatality. Duncan. Elizabeth, I knew, had paid off his student loan and helped to establish him in the business partnership, but that had been all. His placid acceptance that his wife was rich while he was, if not poor, much less well endowed, added to his refusal to accept more than an occasional gift from her, appeared at first glance to be virtuous; but I had wondered sometimes whether any man really was quite so saintly. He fitted all the criteria to be the fraudster. But why would he wish to harm Maurice Cowieson? There was, I supposed, a possibility that the two had been hand in glove or that Cowieson had stumbled across evidence and had to be silenced, but that seemed very unlikely.

If Duncan had been indulging in an extramarital affair, I thought, there would have been more chance of Cowieson, who seemed to have turned sex from a hobby into an obsession, happening on it. What, then, would

Duncan's attitude have been? The risk of a breach with his extremely well-to-do wife might well have driven him to murder. He seemed to be a very mild young man, but the same had been said of many famous murderers.

The builder, Allardyce, seemed a more promising suspect for the murder. If he had discovered, as he inevitably would at some stage, that Maurice Cowieson had given him a worthless guarantee of payment, he might well have been overcome by fury; and a builder is in one of the professions most likely to have blunt but lethal instruments to hand.

The moon had vanished behind a cloud. The clarity of my thoughts was doing much the same. I threw away the butt of the cigar. Another idea had been forming in my mind like a night-time shadow emerging from the mist, which might turn out to be a tree or a horse or a hobgoblin. Before it could take firmer shape, Joanna came out of the house, peering into the dark. The Inspector, she said, would like to see me.

'Waiting for Hamish to fetch you home?' I asked her.

Her smile flashed white in the darkness. 'A keeper can work all the hours God gives,' she said. 'And I've no liking for walking through the woods in the dark. There's nothing to be feared of but you can't help imagining things.' She called Spin to her and vanished in the direction of the kitchen.

Ian and WDC McLure were where I had left them, but neither Elizabeth nor Duncan was to be seen.

'Well?' I said. 'Is it my turn to be suspected of something?'

'We don't suspect you of either crime,' Ian said patiently. He spoiled it by adding, 'You wouldn't have had time for the murder, you don't know enough about electronics and your car has an automatic transmission.'

I tried not to gape at him. His last remark failed altogether to fit in with any of the fragments which I had used as a framework for my thoughts. I had a sudden irrational fear that we might each be talking about several crimes unknown to the other. 'What has my car to do with it?' I asked.

He smiled enigmatically, enjoying my mystification. 'I wanted to ask you to confirm that Elizabeth Ilwand was in the house when you left, before you found the crashed car.'

'Definitely,' I said.

He grunted. 'I'll just have to go back to DCI Dornoch and report progress in a backward direction. He'll be delighted. At least I have an excuse for asking him not to make any more use of my services. I know too many of the witnesses personally – but, apparently, not well enough. Tell me, what's your frank opinion of Mr Duncan Ilwand's character?'

I had been asking myself the same question without arriving at any firm conclusion. 'I've never had reason to believe that he's anything but open and honest. And, in fact, totally laid-back. On the face of it, he's the most relaxed and imperturbable person I ever met.'

'I asked for your frank opinion. You're not being frank, you're qualifying everything you say.'

An hour earlier, out of a sense of duty, I had intended to direct Ian's attention towards Duncan, but now that his attention was on the young man I found myself unwilling to risk focusing it. 'I'm trying to be precise,' I said. 'I haven't seen a great deal of Duncan and he speaks so little that I can't claim to know him. He seems so open and honest that, just before you sent for me, I found myself wondering if he wasn't . . .'

'Too good to be true?'

'Something like that. Can't he account for his movements?' I asked.

I heard Miss McLure give a tiny hiss of surprise at the irregular question but Ian knew me well and took it in his stride. 'He can account for them,' he said. 'So far, the people he met are rather vague about the times. But my colleagues will get there in the end, given a little help.'

'And the builder?' I said. 'Allardyce? I have to be sure who I'm dealing with. In confidence, has he accounted for his movements?'

I had gone too far. Ian drew himself up. WDC McLure closed her notebook with an audible snap. No doubt I was about to be treated to a severe snub. But before it could be delivered we heard the sound of a car on the gravel. It was not being driven particularly fast or carelessly and yet there was something about the rhythm of the driving that disturbed me and I could see that Ian recognized it too.

Joanna was at the door before the visitor could reach it. I heard the mutter of voices and then she appeared at the study door.

'Mr Miles Cowieson wants to speak to you,' she said. She was looking at me.

Miles Cowieson, when he walked into the room, was no longer the brash and self-confident young man from the *après*-shoot party. His healthy outdoor colour seemed to have faded and his manner was hesitant. He picked mine out from the three faces.

'I . . . I've just got back,' he said shakily. 'I went home. There was a policeman there and my home's sealed up. He said that my father's been killed. I'm told that you found him and that you seem to know more about what's going on than anybody else outside the police. I came to find out as much as I can before I see them.'

That information would hardly have come from the policeman left to guard the house. He must have encountered Bea Payne. 'I'm afraid it's all true,' I said. 'You have my condolences. But you're too late to do your homework before you talk to the police. This is Detective Inspector Fellowes and WDC McLure.'

Miles switched his attention to Ian. 'I think I've met your wife,' he said vaguely. 'Are you investigating my father's death?'

'Detective Chief Inspector Dornoch is in charge of the case,' Ian said. 'I'm here on quite another matter. Because I was coming here anyway, it was left to me to clear up certain points concerning your father's death. Mr Dornoch will certainly want to see you.' Ian paused and went on reluctantly. 'But, since we've met up, we may as well get a few preliminary questions out of the way. Do sit down. Where have you been for the last few days?'

Miles lowered himself slowly into a chair. 'I've been in Holland. But I want to know what happened.'

'Were you on holiday?'

'Part of the time,' Miles said. 'I was overdue for a break. I did a year's study around the plant nurseries a few years ago, so I have some friends in Holland and I speak a little of the language. Mostly, I was chasing up finance. My father had . . .' He stopped dead.

'We know about your father's financial difficulties,' Ian said. 'They will be treated in confidence if possible.'

'Yes. But you still haven't told me how he died.'

Ian assumed his stubborn face. I could see another bout of verbal fencing coming up. 'I think,' I said, 'that Mr Cowieson is concerned whether his father may have committed suicide.'

Ian's face cleared. 'There was some question of that but it has been eliminated.'

'Thank God!' Miles said fervently. He breathed deeply. 'My father had run the firm down badly, that has to be admitted. The stockbrokers had turned their backs and any bank loans that he'd been offered would have been crippling. He promised that if I could raise the money to tide us over the serious cash-flow problem, he'd let me have more of a say in the running of the company and digging it out of the red.' He looked back to me again. 'This isn't the best of times to talk business, but I hope to have some good news for you very soon.'

I decided that I would be the judge as to whether his news was good or not. 'Where are you expecting the money to come from?' I asked bluntly.

'I don't think that I need to comment on that. As long as Agrotechnics gets paid . . . Can you tell me what happened to my father? I'm not getting much sense out of these two.'

'I will give you all the sense you can want,' Ian said grittily. 'Mr Kitts found your father's car standing on its nose at the foot of the steep embankment above the Den Burn. Your father was in the driving seat, supported by his seat belt and the air bag. Neither Mr Kitts nor the ambulance staff detected signs of life and he was declared dead at the hospital. His head had suffered fatal damage. At first glance, it looked as if he'd had a blackout or lost concentration and gone straight ahead where the road takes a bend.'

'But you're not satisfied?'

'What makes you say that?'

Miles Cowieson's temper began to fray. The last vestiges of his innate charm vanished and he took on the look of an animal making up its mind to attack. 'If you were bloody satisfied,' he said, 'there wouldn't be a bloody detective chief inspector investigating, plus yourself and Miss McLure and the copper at my house and probably a few bloody dozen others. If you've got to ask questions, at least let them be sensible ones.'

Ian had been doing no more than dangling a little bait, but he could hardly offer that explanation. He pursed his lips. 'No, we're not satisfied, for a number of reasons which I'll go into later. You flew out on Sunday morning?'

'I did. I think . . .' Miles dug in an inner pocket. 'Here's the counterfoil of my ticket.' His eyes narrowed. 'Let's get this straight. Do you think that I killed my father?'

Ian studied the ticket carefully before passing it to WDC McLure. 'I have no opinion on that,' he said before looking up, 'but we wouldn't be doing our duty if we failed to eliminate any doubt. Whoever travelled on this ticket was in the air before your father died. Can you prove that it was you?'

Miles cast up his eyes. 'I showed my passport before getting on the plane,' he said patiently. 'On the plane, I used my credit card to buy a bottle of whisky and some gifts for my Dutch friends. The card has my photograph on it and the slip has my signature. Is that enough?'

'If it checks out. What car do you drive?'

Miles's eyebrows went up but he answered promptly. 'A green Mondeo, two years old.'

'Automatic or manual?'

'Automatic. It's outside if you want to see it.' It was plain that Miles was as puzzled by this turn in the questioning as I was.

'Shortly. Can you think of anyone who would want your father dead?'

Miles locked eyes with Ian for some seconds before deciding that truth came before filial loyalty. 'Dozens who might be pleased that he's dead,' he said. 'Just don't ask me to name them. But I can't think of anybody who'd have killed him. Dad wasn't always too finicky in his business dealings and he was a devil when it came to women.' Miles smiled crookedly. 'Sometimes I wish that I'd inherited a little more of his . . . his brass neck, his machismo. He thought nothing of asking a woman he'd only just met if she fancied a meal and a night of carnal pleasure. It didn't matter if she was married or in a relationship. He got his face slapped a few times but he got a lot of overnight company too. It got so that I had to knock before I went looking for my breakfast. It's embarrassing to walk in on your father and a lady in a state of partial undress. And as far as he was concerned, any such relationship usually ended sharp after breakfast. There must have been a lot of angry husbands and partners, and slighted ladies.'

'We did know most of what you've just told us,' Ian said. 'I apologize for making you live through it again. But we've been looking for these ladies without finding more than one or two.'

'They're hardly likely to advertise,' Miles pointed out.

162

'I couldn't help you. Dad and I went our separate ways outside office hours and moved in different social circles. I recognized very few of the faces, and none of those within the last year or two. Confidentiality is the very essence of hochmagandy, at least in a wee country town like this.'

'That's true.' Ian sounded surprised but I thought that he was faking it.

'I couldn't even offer you any descriptions – I tried to look the other way. Well, wouldn't you?'

Ian's face stiffened as he fought back a smile. 'I sincerely hope,' he said, 'that the situation will never arise.'

'But I still don't understand,' Miles said plaintively. 'If my father was killed in his car near here, why is the house all sealed up?'

'I may as well tell you—'

Miss McLure nudged her superior and looked towards me. I think that Ian had quite forgotten that I was still there.

I said, 'My promise of confidentiality still stands.'

Ian nodded vaguely. His mind was still on dealing with Miles. 'The combined opinions of the pathologist and the forensic science team support the view that your father was struck down elsewhere and immediately put into his car, driven to the nearest suitable piece of road and sent over the embankment. It was very nearly accepted as the accident it was supposed to simulate. I doubt if you'd want to hear any more details just yet.'

'I think that I'm entitled to them,' Miles said doggedly.

Ian hesitated again. I could see his problem. The police practice is for information to be released at the last moment, if at all. Too much openness might give the inimical Detective Chief Inspector some more ammu-

163

nition; too little might provoke a complaint from Miles with the same outcome. I began to see the logic in Ian's policy of keeping his own counsel whenever possible and trying to resolve his cases before Edinburgh became involved.

'Very well,' he said at last. 'We thought at first that your father might have been struck by a vehicle, but a mist of blood spots has been detected on the wall at the side of your house. DNA tests confirm that they were your father's blood. As you know, the old lead pipes across the garden are in process of being replaced. There were several discarded pieces of iron water-pipe around the trench. They tested clean, but we found another piece in the water at the bottom of the trench. Any traces of blood were too faint for DNA typing, but there was a tiny piece of skin trapped in a split in the cut end.'

'And that was his?'

'Yes. Unfortunately, this all seems to have happened after lunch on Sunday, a time when the industrial estate is empty and the roads tend to be at their quietest. If there are any witnesses to say who may have been near your house at that time, we haven't found them yet. So you'll see that, though the assumption is that your father was killed outside the house, we're keeping the interior undisturbed until we know a little more.'

'I understand that,' Miles said.

'If you have any problem about accommodation for the night—'

'No problem there, thank you all the same.' Miles's expression softened. 'Beatrice Payne, who lives in the granny-flat upstairs, heard me speaking with your constable. She came out like the Good Samaritan that she is and offered me the spare bed in her boxroom for the night.' He managed to sound like a paragon of virtue but I was ready to bet that the bed in the boxroom would not see him that night. 'Tomorrow, I'd like access to some of my clothes.'

'That can be arranged.'

Miles shook his head as if to clear it and then turned to me. 'It's a lot to assimilate in a hurry and I'll have to get my mind clear about running the business and getting it back on the rails. I hadn't expected to have to pick up the reins in such a hurry. Could I come and see you tomorrow? I understand from Bea that you saved her bacon in my absence. I'll thank you properly when I see you again.'

'No need for that. I'll come to you,' I said. 'In the morning?'

'Give me until the afternoon. On top of everything else, I'm my father's sole executor. And his heir.'

Ian stiffened. 'Do you have his will?'

'It's kept at the bank.'

'Detective Chief Inspector Dornoch will be wanting a much more detailed statement from you,' Ian told him. 'That will take at least a morning.'

'Then, could we make it Thursday? The day after tomorrow?' Miles asked me.

I had been hoping to wind up my business interests in the area and go home, at least for a few days, but I had no desire to tackle the long drive twice in quick succession. If I could settle matters with Cowieson Farm Supplies, in particular proving to my own satisfaction that any money produced by Miles did not derive from organized crime, another day or two in Newton Lauder might be well spent. I did not intend Agrotechnics to become involved in laundering drug money.

'That should be all right,' I said. 'I'll phone you.'

At a nod from Ian, WDC McLure escorted Miles Cowieson outside and no doubt got a good look at his car. Some secret signal must have passed between them, because she did not come back.

'Is the new man giving you a hard time?' I asked.

Ian shrugged, unsmiling. 'A hard time I could take. What I can't take is him making rotten reports about me to the big cheeses. I've run across him before. Whatever I do is wrong. Do you reckon that Miles Cowieson's alibi will stand up?'

'I'd be prepared to bet on it.'

'I think I just did. If he isn't in the clear, I definitely told him too much. But I had to question him before he could cover up. Didn't I?'

'Of course.' I could see that Ian was only seeking reassurance and trying to convince himself. 'Who does Mr Dornoch suspect?'

Ian looked at his watch and got to his feet. 'Lord, I'd better go,' he said hastily. 'Wendy McLure will be waiting in the car. We were lucky to get her services. She's a real whiz at this computer stuff.'

He hurried out. I went to the door and watched the Land Rover drive away.

I found Elizabeth in the sitting room. She looked up quickly as I came in. 'Did I hear them leave?'

'All gone,' I said. 'Miles Cowieson turned up.'

'Duncan's gone to bed.'

I gave her a summary of what had been said but she listened abstractedly with her eyes out of focus. 'You've got something else on your mind,' I said. 'Cough it up, Gooseberry. You'll feel better.'

She made a grimace. 'Ian Fellowes,' she said. 'I

wouldn't have known him for Deborah's husband. He seemed so hostile.'

'It's his job,' I said. 'Not to be hostile, I don't mean that. But you can't expect him to go easy on anyone just because he knows them socially. Was he accusing you of something?'

'Not me. But he was asking questions about Duncan. When did he go out? Where did he go? And so on and so forth. Some I could answer and about some of them I only knew what Duncan had told me. When he'd finished I went to find Duncan. It was the first time I've ever seen him shaken. He was definitely worried.'

'What had Ian asked him?'

'He didn't get as far as telling me in detail. But he's sure Ian – or that Detective Chief Inspector, whatever his name is – suspects him of killing Maurice Cowieson because he – Duncan – thought that Mr Cowieson had stolen my money. Duncan knew that it couldn't have happened that way but Ian could have thought that he thought that.' Elizabeth paused and frowned. 'Do you follow?'

'I think so,' I said.

'Duncan just kept saying that Mr Cowieson couldn't use a computer to save his life. Duncan went along to the office to fix something in Miles's computer and Miles's father told him he "couldn't be doing with all this modern fiddle-faddle". But Duncan was sure that Ian thought he was making it up.'

'Ian's not so easily fooled,' I said weakly. 'But Mr Cowieson Senior doesn't seem to have had a high regard for the truth. He may have told somebody else that he was a computer genius.'

Elizabeth was hardly taking in a word I was saying.

'But what about this Detective Chief Inspector?' she demanded. 'Dornoch is it? He may be the one who thinks that Duncan's guilty.'

'They probably don't think any such thing,' I pointed out. 'It's one of their ways of working. They throw a lot of accusations around and see who reacts. Anyway, thinking and proving are a long, long way apart.'

'I suppose so.' Elizabeth was looking stressed beyond endurance. She drew a long and shuddering breath. I guessed that we were arriving at the nub of her worries. 'Ian asked me what Duncan's attitude was to having married a rich woman. He didn't quite ask out loud whether Duncan had married me for my money, but very nearly.' I saw that there were tears in her eyes. 'Uncle Henry, what do *you* think?'

'I think that he's probably asking similarly provocative questions of a whole lot of people,' I said. 'It goes with the job.'

She shook her head miserably. 'No, no. I mean about Duncan. Is he really . . . I mean . . .?'

I broke in to spare her any more embarrassment. 'You mean, is he too good to be true?' (Elizabeth nodded without speaking.) 'I think we've all been wondering that, perhaps because he really is so free from envy that we weaker mortals find it difficult to believe him. You should know him better than anybody. You knew him at university. And you've married him. Was he always so laid-back? So content with his lot?'

Elizabeth half closed her eyes. As she recalled her courtship days she even smiled. 'Yes, I think he was. It didn't seem to bother him that he never had two pennies to rub together. Well, none of us did. Some of us—' she flushed suddenly ' – yes, like me, some of us became rebels and made our parents' lives a misery. And grand-parents.'

'Come off it, Gooseberry,' I said. 'You never made your grandfather miserable. He loved you dearly right up to the end. And Duncan has never shown any sign of grudging you your money. He even refused a settlement. I can't reconcile that with him resenting anything. If he did, you'd have known before anybody else did. But, be fair, you never thought about it until Ian Fellowes put the thought into your head.'

'But that's what's so awful,' she said in a choked voice. 'It did enter my head. Duncan never behaved any way except perfectly but I couldn't help wondering, now and again . . .'

She got to her feet and bolted out of the room. A little later, I heard her go up to bed.

I thought that I had put her doubts out of my mind, but I woke up suddenly in the night to the recognition of Elizabeth's real worry. Duncan's refusal of a marriage settlement might be the action of an honourable and unworldly man. But there was another possible explanation. He could have been playing for higher stakes. There had been many examples in history of men who had married for money and in due course killed their brides.

Chapter Eight

As it developed, the Wednesday of that week was so taken up with other discussions that I would have had no time to fit in another with Miles Cowieson.

First, Ralph Enterkin wanted a word with me and rather more than a word. I could combine that visit with another trip to Edinburgh, so I borrowed Ronnie and the Range Rover again and went down to Ralph's dusty office in a tall, stone building overlooking the Square in Newton Lauder. As fellow trustee, he had a right to be apprised of everything which might possibly affect Elizabeth and the estate. The health of Agrotechnics undoubtedly fell within that definition so that it was necessary, while honouring my promise to Ian by reminding Ralph of the confidentiality of the trustee-to-ward relationship, to spell out all that I knew about both the murder and the fraud.

'You're going to have to call up the floating charge,' he said when I had finished.

'We gave his father a fortnight,' I said. 'In writing. It may not be legally necessary, but it seems only fair to give his heir the same margin.'

'If he comes up with the money—'

'He'd better have a damned good explanation of where it came from,' I finished for him.

He pulled the extraordinary face which, with him,

accompanies deep thought. 'Oh dear, oh dear!' he said. 'It seems highly probable that one of my clients will be charged with the murder.'

This was interesting. Could Ralph really be so far ahead of the rest of us? 'Which one?' I asked.

'I don't know which one,' he said testily, 'and if I knew I could hardly tell you. These people are nearly all clients of mine – except for the unfortunate Maurice Cowieson, who isn't around any more. I seem to remember defending him from a drunk driving charge many years ago, but since then my acquaintance with him has been limited to pursuing him on behalf of young – and some not-so-young – ladies who have felt themselves to be wronged and negotiating a settlement when possible. Sadly, breach of promise suits are almost impossible in today's climate, so that it was usually necessary to make mention of such matters as indecent assault.' He frowned absently. 'What was I talking about? I seem to have strayed.'

'You were telling me – or not telling me – which of your clients you expect to be charged with murder.'

'I'll have a better idea as soon as one of them phones for an urgent appointment.'

My years in banking taught me the knack of reading upside down. It had been very useful on occasions when some plausible character had been trying to obtain more credit than he was worth. Ralph's diary was open on the desk and for early that afternoon I could make out an entry. Allardyce, it read.

When we had exhausted our discussion, Ralph wanted me to join him for lunch – at the expense of the estate, of course – but I made my excuses and escaped to the Range Rover. I had other fish to poach – literally, because the pub that we stopped at for lunch had some quite respectable fresh salmon on the menu despite the approach of the breeding season.

I invited Ronnie to join me at table. Servants often know more of what is going on than their masters. I asked him what news and rumours he had heard.

'Deil a word,' he said. 'They haud their gabs while I'm around.' He scowled ferociously. 'They'd bloody better. I'll no stand for gibble-gabble aboot the mistress. But I've een in ma heid. Yestreen, I was in the Canal Bar wi Mary. Allardyce the builder cam in an nae bugger wad look at his skook. There wis neither hishie nor wishie gin he turned and went oot.'

If the denizens of the Canal Bar fell silent and looked away when Allardyce entered, there must be some word going around, but whether that had to do with being defrauded, or murder, or something new I was damned if I could guess.

'How do you get on with Mr Ilwand?' I asked him.

We had known each other before Duncan came on the scene, so Ronnie was prepared to be quite open. 'He's a guid lad,' he said. 'He suits the mistress fine.'

'He seems very relaxed, very laid back,' I said. 'Most husbands would feel awkward or even envious if their wives had all the money but it doesn't seem to embarrass him at all. Or is that just a front?'

'Not a bit of it.' Ronnie shook his head. 'He disna gie a damn aboot siller. When he's few pounds in's pootch, he buys the mistress a wee gift. He'll hae a birthday suin an the mistress was axing him whit he'd like an he couldna think on a thing. She wis ettling tae gie him another motor. She asked would he no like to tak her car and she'd get a new yin but he said he wis used wi the

172

yin he's got an, oniewey, he couldna get on wi automatic gears.'

'He'll be carried up to heaven on a pale pink cloud, one of these days,' I said. Being impatient and short-tempered and not having always been virtuous (until advancing years made any other course barely worth the energy required), I sometimes feel that excessive virtue is a waste of good temptation.

I had a doze in the back of the Range Rover during the rest of the journey to Edinburgh.

My session with Gordon Bream was even more exhausting than that with Ralph Enterkin. Gordon was doubly interested in the well-being of Agrotechnics. I was able to assure him again that Elizabeth would easily meet her obligations. His only interest in the death of Maurice Cowieson was its possible effect on Cowieson Farm Supplies Ltd and thus indirectly on Agrotechnics. Word had, as usual, found its way into the media and the fact that the apparently accidental death was under investigation by the police was known. DCI Dornoch, fortunately, when pressed for a statement, had managed to hint that the interest of the police was in such questions as whether dangerous driving or sloppy vehicle maintenance might be to blame, so that media interest was at a very low level.

Gordon, however, was not put off by such red herrings and I had the difficult task of outlining the legal position and probable prospects without quite breaking my promise to Ian. Fortunately, Ralph Enterkin had read me a lecture which increased my rudimentary appreciation of the legalities and I was able to persuade Gordon to adhere to my plan, giving Miles Cowieson the remainder of the period we had allowed his father, leaving him in

charge meantime. We would look very hard at the origins
of any money that he produced, failing which we would
call up the floating charge. Whether we would continue
Miles's employment as sales manager could be decided
in the light of his performance in the interim, but I had
brought with me Miles's list of proposals for injecting
fresh life into Cowieson Farm Supplies Ltd. We also
agreed, reluctantly, that Cowieson's debt to McQueen and
Allardyce would have to be settled.

It was time to regularize the decisions we had made in
the names of our fellow directors. We produced a minute
confirming our decisions, prepared formal notes to Colin
Weir and to Agrotechnics confirming the position and
tidied up the remainder of the paperwork. Maintaining a
perfect record of transactions and decisions may be
tedious and usually a total waste of time but, when things
go wrong and the lawyers move in, such a record can be
worth far more than its weight in paper money.

At last I was free and Ronnie drove me back to
Newton Lauder. As we slowed to turn off the main road,
I glanced incuriously at a small police car which had
stopped at the junction and was waiting for the traffic to
clear. As we made our turn, the lights of an oncoming
coach played into the car and I saw that the driver was
WDC McLure. It look me a second to recognize her. She
was in uniform, very spruce. The poor light made it
difficult to be sure but an improvement in her appearance
suggested that she was carefully but discreetly made up.
A gap opened and I heard tyres yelp as she spurted out.
Turning my head I saw that the blue light was flashing
and she was bullying her way through the traffic.

I had telephoned to say that I would be late. Elizabeth
and Duncan had already eaten dinner but Elizabeth

came and sat with me and even accepted a glass of wine while I picked at a piece of Dover sole. I am as fond of fish as the next man but twice in a day is too much.

Elizabeth was more cheerful than I had seen her since the evening of the shoot. The reason was soon clear. 'Ian was on the phone. He's coming tonight. He says that that Woman Detective Constable has made amazing progress today. He says that she's a real ball of fire and he was very lucky to get her.'

'He said much the same to me,' I told her. 'I just hope that she doesn't burn out before she's tracked your money down. She passed us, going towards Edinburgh like a bat out of hell. She was in uniform but all prettied up.'

Elizabeth's expression soured for a moment. 'Going to make eyes at another lot of officers I suppose,' she said.

'And the best of luck to her,' I retorted. If WDC McLure had found good reason to make herself smart and presentable before returning to Edinburgh, it could only be to further the case in hand; or so I hoped.

I could see that Elizabeth was putting an altogether less charitable interpretation on my last words, but her manner implied that she had more important topics to discuss than the amours of a junior police officer. 'Ian has to go to a briefing with the senior man from Edinburgh, so he can't come to us until later in the evening. A nuisance for him – he can't be seeing much of Deborah just now – but it fits quite well, because Mrs Ombleby rang up. She wants to see me this evening.' Elizabeth looked at her watch. 'She'll be here soon. Do you want to meet her?'

I did rather want to see Mrs Ombleby again. Her name had been linked to that of the late Maurice

Cowieson and I thought that I might get that gentleman's amorous adventures into better perspective if I could gently sound out one of his targets. And if Elizabeth was contemplating an investment in Mrs Ombleby's project I would certainly want to sit in on their discussion.

The lady arrived in the XJS drophead Jaguar which had belonged to her late husband – and which I definitely coveted, although Isobel would have suspected the most immoral motives if I had ever contemplated purchasing such a car. On the day of the shoot I had seen Mrs Ombleby in the roughest of tweed and, only an hour later, in navy silk and well chosen but undoubtedly valuable jewellery. Now she had taken the middle road, a severe working dress with little make-up and the only jewellery was on her marriage finger. Then, she had been one of the many background figures. Looking at her with fresh eyes, I saw that she was well rounded, verging on stout, but in the firm and bouncing way that makes the fatness neither a burden to its bearer nor an eyesore but rather a hint of jollity. She smelled, very faintly, expensive. Her hair, which had been tinted back to its original brown, had been styled by an expensive hand but was now worn loose. Her features were strong but slightly blurred, her eyes keen. She was, I noticed, light on her feet. The overall effect was of a woman of energy and intelligence, and one who still had much to offer to a man such as the late Mr Cowieson.

Elizabeth brought her to the study where I was waiting and reminded each of us of the other's identity. Mrs Ombleby shook hands like a man and favoured me with a smile. We settled in the deep, leather chairs. 'We spoke on Saturday,' she said. 'You were the hero of the hour. And I believe that you're one of Elizabeth's trustees.'

So time was not to be wasted in idle chatter. I approved of that in a busy woman. 'Only for a few more months,' I said.

'But until then, you're standing by to make sure that nobody puts anything over on her?' The words were spoken without ulterior meaning. 'Very wise. Elizabeth tells me that she's let you in on my secret. What's your first impression?'

'It sounds like a brainwave,' I said. 'And the moment seems to be propitious, now that electronic shopping is coming in.'

She looked at me closely, to see if I was only making polite noises. 'As a man, you may not appreciate the drag on a busy woman of having to think up the menus, translate them into ingredients and quantities and make a long list. Internet shopping, as it's being planned at the moment, will take it from there to the point where she has to follow the proper recipe for each bit of each meal.'

'And that's the point at which you find that you've run out of something,' I said. 'I know. My wife's a busy vet and dog trainer and I have to help out for much of the time. Sadly, we live away out in the country, so it may be years before we can benefit from your service. But I love the idea of shopping by formula and receiving the right ingredients packaged along with the recipe. Working wives and harassed mums will love it too.'

'But you don't sound convinced.'

I was surprised that she could detect any note of reserve in my voice. I was weighing the project up as an investment, but on the whole I was ready to be convinced. 'I'm only wondering how much it will cost,' I said.

She nodded slowly and gravely. 'Not as much as you'd think. Of course, we may be beyond the means of the single parent on Social Security or the student in a flat; but most people are better off than ever before and prepared to spend money to make life easier for themselves. The cost of delivery is partly offset by the saving in using warehouse space instead of expensive high street shopping space. With the help of a good computerized system, the extra cost of breaking down the purchases into dish ingredients and furnishing the recipe is almost negligible.' From a folder, she produced some cost figures and I ran my eye over them. She had been thorough and she answered my few questions without hesitation.

'And you're looking for finance?'

She met my eye frankly. 'Mostly, I'm financing the first phase, in Edinburgh and Glasgow, myself. That's how much faith I have in the idea. If it fails, I'm wiped out, but that's my problem. If it works as I think it will and we go nationwide, then I'll need more capital.'

'I've been telling Mrs Ombleby that I may not be able to invest after all,' Elizabeth said. She sounded almost guilty.

'Things are looking healthier,' I told her. 'If you want to invest, subject only to results in the first phase looking good, I think you could give Mrs Ombleby an assurance. If by any chance we don't raise enough capital, I'll find some bridging money for you.'

They both smiled at me. Mrs Ombleby began to gather her papers, but I had not yet satisfied my curiosity. 'Have you come far?' I asked.

She snapped the lock on her briefcase and sat back, prepared to devote a few finite minutes to the courtesies. 'Five or six miles. I live just outside the town, to the south.'

So she had been almost a neighbour of Maurice

Cowieson. 'Did you come through the town or up the back road?' I asked her.

Her eyebrows went up. 'I didn't know that there was a back road or I'd have used it. They have Main Street up again, with cones and barriers and temporary traffic lights and not a sign of anybody actually doing anything.'

'Then you'd certainly have saved time on the back road. You turn off beside the industrial estate. Behind where Maurice Cowieson lived,' I said without emphasis.

For a moment I saw an expression on her face which was hard to interpret. It was neither fear nor anger but, I thought, distaste. Then Mrs Ombleby looked at the carriage clock over the fireplace. 'I must be going,' she said. 'If I turn right outside the archway, will that take me up to the back road?'

We promised that it would.

'Then I'll go that way and I'll know it next time. We'll keep in touch.' She shook hands with me again and Elizabeth went to the door with her.

'You shouldn't have mentioned Mr Cowieson,' Elizabeth said, returning to the study when the Jaguar had oozed away. 'It's a sensitive subject.'

'Did they ... have something going?' I asked, choosing the most contemporary metaphor that I could think of in order to keep the question light.

She hid a smile. 'I shouldn't think so. She thought that he was a crook. She came here last week and asked me if I'd told anybody about her plans. I told her that I hadn't and I insisted on her telling me why she thought I might have done. She said that somebody must have spilled the beans because Maurice Cowieson had approached her. He knew all about it.'

'He could have stumbled on some of your e-mails in the Internet,' I suggested.

'Mr Cowieson couldn't have found his way into the Internet if they'd left the door open,' Elizabeth said contemptuously. 'You heard Duncan say so, more or less. But he'd got hold of it somehow and he was threatening to sell the idea to one of the big food wholesalers.'

'He wanted money?'

'Not exactly,' Elizabeth said. She paused, either to build up the drama or while she wondered whether I was fit to hear more secrets. But there was a happy glint in her eye. The scandal was too good to keep. 'He wanted sex.'

'Did he get it?' I asked before I could check myself.

'She said not.'

It hardly bore wondering about. Any mental picture of Maurice Cowieson's skinny frame in juxtaposition with Mrs Ombleby's rich curves was faintly repugnant. I decided to change the subject quickly. 'Wouldn't she really know about the back road?' I asked.

Elizabeth lost interest. 'I'd have thought so,' she said.

We did not have to wait long for Ian. This time, he came alone. He looked tired. He was much less formal, now that murder was not on the agenda. It seemed that we were now on the same side. 'I almost wish that I hadn't borrowed that woman from Edinburgh,' he said. 'She seems to have the knack of doing fourteen things simultaneously, several of which consist of driving me towards the same sort of energy output. I only asked for her because she'd been on the same course on computer fraud and seemed to ask the right questions. It turns out that she knows almost everybody. She has degrees in both computing and physics and all the energy of an atomic pile. And like a pile, she irritates. I suppose that Edinburgh were glad to get a short respite from her. She's totally exhausted me and I never even laid a finger on her.'

'And that would have been all right, would it?' Elizabeth demanded, her feminist hackles rising. 'Being exhausted because you *had* laid a finger on her?'

'I was joking,' Ian explained patiently. 'Deborah would have seen it. But never mind. When she wasn't setting tasks for me, WDC McLure spent much of the day on the phone. She always seemed to know the right person to speak to and now she's gone into Edinburgh to get hold of somebody senior who can lean on people in the telephone and banking industries to find and cough up some more information which is not usually disgorged.

'Our target thinks that he or she – let's stick to *he* for the sake of simplicity – has been very clever. In point of fact, he *has* been rather clever, he'd have beaten me hands down. But Miss McLure had it pinned down in minutes. It helped that his service provider – Demon – is now owned by Scottish Telecom. The service providers, of course, are only too anxious to see the frauds which are being carried out in their names stopped.' He looked at Elizabeth. 'So they helped us to trace the method by which their charges had been paid. After all, even when they thought that our man was innocent they weren't going to let him use their facilities without getting paid for it. It turned out that he'd given them a direct debit authority on an account with an Edinburgh branch of the Royal Bank which had been opened over the phone the previous week in the name of Roger Breeks and giving an address which doesn't exist. According to the bank, somebody came in and deposited two hundred pounds in used Clydesdale tenners and that was that. Nobody has the faintest recollection as to what he looked like and the security video only shows a slightly out-of-focus figure in a plain mackintosh and a hat with a downturned brim, heavy spectacles and a bushy moustache which is almost certainly false.

'So Demon set about tracing the origin of the e-mail which reached you and the destination of the one which you sent back.' He paused. 'The originating computer was the mainframe at Agrotechnics.' I jumped and I must have made a sound of surprise, because he laughed silently. 'Don't let that weigh too much with you. The e-mail reached the Agrotechnics computer from a mobile phone over a satellite link, hooked presumably to a laptop computer, and was sent on automatically.'

'So that's a dead end?' Elizabeth suggested.

'Only for the moment. We've got the number of the mobile, but that was bought over the phone, paid for and connected in the name of the same Mr Breeks. We've no way of knowing where that phone is now although we may be able to trace it if any more calls are made from it. More likely it's been chucked on the back of somebody's fire. But we know that when it sent the original e-mail and received your reply it was in this cell area. As a matter of interest, another reply has been sent to it, so presumably there was another, um . . .' On the point of uttering some such word as mug or sucker, Ian caught himself. 'Victim,' he said carefully. 'Whoever that may be either hasn't noticed the loss yet or doesn't want to appear . . . unwise, because it hasn't been reported yet.'

'And is that as far as we can get?' I asked.

'Our target may think so. It's as far as we've got so far,' Ian said. 'As I told you, Miss McLure's gone in to Edinburgh to get support from somebody closer to Chief Constable level. We want your bank to trace where the money was transferred to or, if they still won't play ball, the Bank Automated Clearing System in Reading should be able to do it.'

'In that case, we've got him?' I suggested.

Ian made a face. 'It won't be that easy. He's been so evasive that he surely won't have left a strong connection between himself and the money. He'll have turned it into something as portable as a banker's draft, maybe several, and carried it to another bank, maybe even another country, and made a fresh deposit.'

'Even a banker's draft could be traced in the end,' I said.

'Think about jewellery, drugs, antiques, rare postage stamps. Laundering has been brought to a fine art in recent years. But don't lose heart. We'll see what tomorrow brings.'

'Suppose it brings the information we're looking for,' Elizabeth said. 'Suppose word comes back that the culprit was Charlie Buggins in Newton Lauder. What then?'

Ian sighed. 'Then we start all over again. We may be able to prove that he committed the fraud. If he decides to hold his tongue, we have to find what he did with the money. We may have to point out to him that judges go very hard on villains who could make restitution but don't. If he denies that the Rembrandt painting in his wife's safe deposit box was acquired with your money, we may have to set out to prove it all over again. You may even have to sue him for the return of your million-plus.'

183

'It goes on for ever, doesn't it?' Elizabeth said dully.

'It can do,' Ian said. 'Justice is not a very fast-moving lady. But I never told you that it was going to be quick or easy, did I?'

'Quite the reverse,' I said. We seemed to have exhausted the subject of fraud for the moment so I decided to chance my luck. 'Has Mr Dornoch being giving you more trouble?' I asked.

Ian bridled. I thought that he was going to turn back into the formal police officer addressing one who was a mere member of the public and therefore by definition (in the police dictionary) an ignorant and unreasonable nuisance. But his sense of grievance was too strong. 'That man,' he said, 'is driving me mad. He's more interested in catching me out than in running an investigation.'

'Not the best way to solve a crime,' I suggested.

'He thinks that he has it solved,' Ian said. 'In absolute, total confidence, I think he intends to make an arrest in the morning. And, to our shame, he'll be doing it on the basis, largely, of information furnished by you and relayed by me.'

A quick mental review of the information which I had passed on to Ian assured me that he would not be talking so openly if Duncan had been the target, and I had made no mention of Mrs Ombleby. The next most likely person to leap to mind was . . .

'Mr Allardyce? The builder?' I said.

Clearly, Ian had had no intention of letting that particular cat out of the bag, but he nodded in spite of himself.

'Allardyce,' I said, 'was flabbergasted when I told him that his floating charge was worth rather less than the paper it was written on. And I'm assured that he's a rotten actor.'

Ian nodded again. 'But he's also a rotten driver,' he said. 'And he wouldn't be short of men to come and give him a lift home or down to Cowieson's house to collect his own car. There was a call at about the right time from his mobile to the pub where some of his men were watching the live broadcast of the match on Sky TV instead of waiting for the repeat. The men all deny that the call had anything to do with transport but say it was to give some orders for the next morning's jobs.'

'And the Detective Chief Inspector doesn't believe them?'

Ian grunted. 'The man's a conspiracy theorist.'

'That's as may be,' I said, 'but he doesn't have to rely on proving that the murderer had an accomplice. If his car was still at Cowieson's house, the killer could easily have walked down the hill.'

'My men couldn't find anything significant along the Den Burn,' Ian said, frowning. 'And he'd have been taking an awful risk, with my father-in-law using ferrets nearby and God knows who else about the fields.'

It seemed very unlikely that the builder would have known that Keith was ferreting in the neighbourhood and he evidently knew that most of the male population was watching the match, but it was not for me to offer arguments to the police. I had disliked the builder but I was far from convinced of his guilt. I held my peace and Ian left soon afterwards.

Chapter Nine

Miles Cowieson came on the phone before I had finished breakfast next morning, to suggest an appointment that afternoon. I had hoped to conclude any business that could not be conducted by post or telephone and to get back for a spell to my own bed and board, my own chairs and a television mostly under my own control. I was being made extremely comfortable but I hankered for home, more familiar company and my old routine; and I was sure that I was putting on weight which would soon take its toll of my shopworn hips and knees. The leaner diet at home and Three Oaks, with the accompanying regime and all the walking entailed, was overdue.

That thought brought another in its wake. A good walk might give the vague ideas which were making shifting patterns in my mind a chance to take shape.

I sought Elizabeth out to explain my forthcoming absence. At my age, one should always tell someone exactly where one is going, in case one fails to return. I was unhappy with the police theory that the murderer had been collected by an accomplice. I had not heard the car go down the embankment, but there would surely have been some delay before the killer made his departure. He would no doubt have preferred to set fire to the wreck and only abandoned that plan when he heard me calling the dog. There was no sign that he had struggled up the embankment above the crashed car; he would have had to come towards me to find a place where the bank could be climbed quickly and silently. I was fairly sure that by then I would have been close enough to hear a car driving off. I clung to my original belief that the murderer would have walked back to the Cowieson house by way of the Den Burn.

If I followed what I assumed to have been the path taken by the killer of Maurice Cowieson, I would see what he had seen and I might somehow obtain an insight into his mind and methods. 'I'll walk down the Den Burn,' I said.

Elizabeth had been studying the plans for a new access road to Potter's Farm. She looked up, frowning absently. 'Have you got your mobile?' she asked. 'You can always phone Duncan for a lift back at lunchtime.'

I patted my pocket in confirmation. 'I think I'll take Spin with me.'

'Good idea. Do you want a gun?'

The question was a natural one. Almost all of the route was on land owned by the estate and there was always pressure to keep up the control of rabbits and woodpigeon, but I had no wish to arrive in Newton Lauder armed, even if the gun was bagged. I declined the offer.

Spin, the spaniel, was in the kitchen but he jumped up as soon as I called him. The old Labrador began to struggle to his feet but was easily persuaded to settle again. He had come to recognize his own limitations and to accept that some walks were beyond him. Out of fellow feeling, I decided that I would take him for a stroll on my return. I collected my cap and a stick from the hall and we set off along the drive.

At the old stone archway, which was almost the only remnant of the earlier buildings, I paused. I had already explored the upstream part of the gully as far as the crash site. The murderer, knowing that I was down in the valley bottom, would have walked along the road verge – unless, that is, the police were correct in assuming that he had been picked up by an accomplice.

The burn passed under the drive through a culvert too small for a walker to pass, but on the downstream side a ragged path worn by generations of gamekeepers and dog-walkers descended the steep bank and followed the side of the burn towards Newton Lauder.

I climbed down with care between the dead bracken and gorse bushes and set off along the rough path. The dank weather had relented at last and the sun had come out. The silver birches were already bare but the other hardwoods were in full autumn colour. There were still berries on every bush and overwintering birds were busy building up their reserves for the cold weather to come. The migrants had already departed but the geese had arrived and I watched and listened as a skein passed high overhead until the sound was lost in the chuckle of the burn. Spin had given me a reproachful glance when he saw that I was not carrying a gun but he fell anyway into the to-and-fro search pattern of a working spaniel, quartering the narrow valley and its banks.

My legs, for once, were moving freely and the feel of the day was good. I was busily enjoying myself rather than thinking while half my mind still watched for any-thing which might have seemed significant to the killer. Spin pushed a woodcock out of the cover. It flitted and was gone in a moment on silent wings. I saw him nose one or two scraps of rubbish and then ignore them. He was usually a game-or-nothing dog.

The valley widened for a hundred yards. At one time, a house had stood there and there was still the remains of a track down from the road and a strip remaining of an old kitchen garden wall, higher than my head. There were still a few apples on an old tree which overhung the wall.

It was cold in the shade. But for that, while the mysteries would still have been solved in the end, I might not have played my part.

From the films and novels, you might think that nobody ever had to go to the toilet. The truth, however, is far different, especially when the years have played havoc with your prostate gland. I became aware that I was desperate for a pee. I glanced about me. There were trees around and the little valley's sides were topped with hedges. I could hardly have been more private, so I squared up to the old remnant of garden wall.

Suddenly a voice said 'Hello,' jerking me out of my reverie. A girl's voice, I thought. The sound came out of nowhere. There was no chance of arresting the flow and to turn around would have made all worse. I looked around and back over my shoulder and then up. Only when I raised my eyes did I see a figure perched on the limb of a beechtree overhead. A boy, I was relieved to realize.

'Hello.' I replied. I waited until I was finished and decently zipped before I turned. 'School closed? Or are you playing truant?' Man to man talk, to cover my embarrassment.

'I've been ill,' he said. 'But I'm going back on Monday.

We were just starting Latin, too, so I've missed a bit. We'd just done *Amo, amas.* My Latin teacher, Mr Ghent, was teaching us about declensions or conjugations or something. He told us a poem about *Amo, amas, I love a lass,* but I didn't understand much of it. Do you know any more?' He was a well spoken lad with only the faintest trace of the local accent.

'Try *Flymo, flymas, I cut the grass*,' I suggested.

He laughed loudly, which was gratifying. 'That's very funny,' he said. He slithered suddenly down the tree, lithe as a squirrel, and came to rest on another branch closer to my level. He had been neatly and cleanly dressed but his clothes were suffering from contact with the tree. His mother was going to have something to say. 'I'd have let you go by, but when you stopped there I thought I'd make you jump. I did make you jump. Didn't I?'

'You certainly did.' My mind clicked suddenly into gear. 'Were you here on Sunday?' I asked him.

'No,' he said. I gave a mental shrug. It had been a long shot. 'The police asked me that,' he added.

My interest stirred again. 'Why?'

'They were asking lots of people. I told them I was at home. I live in the white house at the top of the road. They asked if I'd seen anything unusual and I said I hadn't but I told them about the car. It was a little bit unusual.'

'How was it unusual?'

'I see a lot of cars up there but they don't do what this one did. It came as if it had come up the other way from the town. When it was still about as far from the junction as from here to that rock in the middle of the burn—' he pointed to a conspicuous rock a good sixty yards away ' – it suddenly made a great noise of tyres as if something had run out in front of it. But there wasn't anything,' he said earnestly. 'I could see there wasn't. Then it speeded up again and slowed down normally to go round the corner.'

'You mean,' I said, 'that it stood on its nose as if somebody had stamped on the brakes?'

'That's what the policeman asked and I said that I thought that's what it was. You can still see the black marks on the road. I showed them to him.'

When we turned towards the town, the white house was on our left. 'If you were at home,' I said, 'you'd have been on the driver's side of the car.'

'I couldn't see him, if that's what you were going to ask. The car had darkened windows.'

Spin sent up a cock pheasant, rocketing into the sunshine. We watched it out of sight in respectful silence. 'And the driver's window was up?' I asked.

'Yes.'

'What kind of car was it?'

'I didn't see the make,' he said. 'But it was big and that sort of dark red I think they call maroon.'

'Did any other cars go by at about the same time?'

'That was the only one all morning. Would your dog like an apple? Because there's one on top of the wall. Why would anybody put an apple on top of a wall?'

'I don't know,' I said. I reached up, following his directions, and took it down – an ordinary looking, green apple. Tooth-marks in it were turning brown. I put it in my pocket.

I thanked the boy. I would have slipped him a pound, but the days have gone by when you could give somebody else's child money without being suspected of all sorts of evil intentions. I left him in his tree, declining aloud the Latin verb *Flymo*.

My mind might have wandered again but a few hundred yards further on, where we were emerging onto more level ground and the valley was growing shallower, Spin broke his own habit and brought me a scrap of rubbish. I thanked him and put it away carefully. I usually have one or two polythene bags in my pocket, for lifting the occasional dog-plonk which gets deposited on a pavement.

Suddenly I saw the significance of Ian's questions about cars. The pattern in my mind snapped into shape.

I could see the road ahead and the industrial estate. It would soon be the fifth of November and the foundation of a large bonfire was already established in the field beyond the road. This would be the site for the municipal fireworks display, designed to keep bonfires and explosives safely outside the town. Thinking of Guy Fawkes, I was reminded that there is no point having a good idea if you can't carry it through.

I took out my mobile phone and called Ian's number. Several different voices tried to tell me that Ian was busy and offered to take messages but eventually Ian came on the line. 'We've got a little further with your fraud case,' he said at once. 'In the previous cases, the money went from Canada to the Orient and vanished from there, but your ward's money was transferred to a Dutch bank. Does that surprise you?'

'Not in the least,' I said. 'The Dutch banks are more secretive even than the Swiss. It's just where somebody would go to break a trail. And it completes a pattern. If you and WDC McLure care to meet me at Cowieson Farm

Supplies right away, I may be able to point you in the direction of some useful evidence.'

There was a momentary silence. 'All right,' he said at last. 'I'll trust you. Your pointers have been valuable in the past. Ten minutes.'

My path dipped and I lost sight of the buildings. They must have done the trip in less than ten minutes because, when my path emerged again from the gully, the Cowieson buildings were beside me and Ian was just emerging from his police Range Rover in front of the offices. I waved and he acknowledged the signal. I had to skirt the back of the house, cross the still open trench for the new water-pipe and follow the chain link fence round to the entrance to Cowieson Farm Supplies Ltd. Ian stood beside the driver's door of the Range Rover and Miss McLure got out from the front passenger seat as I arrived. They were both in plain clothes. It would have been customary for the more junior officer to do the driving. Another small connection linked up for me. Spin nosed Ian's leg but ignored the WDC.

'Now,' Ian said, 'what's this about?'

When I phoned Ian, I knew exactly what I was going to do and why. As we had disconnected I had begun to worry whether I was going the right way about it. The proper course of action, at least in the view of the police, would have been to visit Ian in his lair, tell him of my suspicions and leave him to accept or discard my theories and investigate what little evidence I had. The problem was that I had very little to go on; just a hunch based on the fit of the parts. In a sense it was like being confronted by an unfamiliar machine in a dismantled state and being required to assemble the parts correctly simply because they wouldn't go together any other way. To complicate the issue further, his objective and mine were similar but not identical.

I had to make up my mind. I wanted to get it all over and go home, so I decided to stick to my original plan and rush in – like any other fool. 'I have one or two questions for the management,' I said. 'My questions may produce evidence of use to you. At any rate, your presence should lend an element of formality to the proceedings.'

Ian looked unhappy. 'If this is just a trick to bolster your leverage . . .' he began.

'We can make it plain that you're impartial,' I said.

Ian hesitated and then gave a nod. They followed me up the single step and into the building. Behind the counter, Bea Payne was standing in the doorway to what had once been Maurice Cowieson's office, speaking to the secretary/receptionist. They both looked at us enquiringly. Spin gave a soft bark, dived round the counter and jumped up against Bea – a greeting which was generally forbidden and which he reserved for her alone. She gave him a quick pat and he returned to my heel.

My mind went blank and then recovered. I decided on an oblique approach. 'When do you expect Miles Cowieson back in the office?' I asked.

'He came back a few minutes ago,' Bea said. 'Rather pleased with himself. He took a very good order from the Penthillan estate.'

With that, the other office door opened and Miles looked out. 'I thought I heard voices,' he told me. 'I wasn't expecting you until this afternoon but we can talk now.' He glanced at the two officers and his bright cheeriness dimmed a little. 'I was hoping for a private talk.'

'They're only here to observe,' I said. 'They want background on your father's business life.'

'I suppose it's all right. You'd better come in. Come with us, Bea.' Ian backed into the office where I had spoken with Bea Payne. We followed. The second desk had been removed and replaced by cheap but comfortable chairs. The drift of papers around the computer was the scattered disorder of a man's desk rather than the orderly clutter of a woman. Miles settled behind the desk and we took chairs. 'The plan is that Miss Payne will be responsible for business management from here on in,' he said. 'I'll do the selling.'

'That's about what I would have expected,' I told him.

Miles leaned forward with his elbows on the desk, rubbing his hands, the light of the fanatic in his eyes. 'I'm going to pull out all the stops to clear the backlog of stock and get the whole business on a proper footing. We've moved quite a lot already simply by treating all enquiries seriously and following them through, which is more than my father ever did. He expected his customers to keep chasing him, begging him to sell them the machinery as a favour, but life isn't like that any more. We're just getting out a mailshot to all the farmers, promising discounts, special terms and a much improved after-sales service. After that, we're hoping that Agrotechnics will join us in some serious promotional ideas along the lines of the action plan which I left with you.'

There was only one way to check his bubbling enthusiasm. 'We may consider it,' I said, 'when Agrotechnics has called up the floating charge and taken over.'

He looked at me with hurt amazement, as though I had farted during the National Anthem. 'But there's no longer any case for that,' he said patiently, as though talking to an infant. 'I wanted this meeting so that I could tell you that I'm in a position to settle the outstanding

Agrotechnics accounts at last. The money came through this morning.' His voice was meant to be confident but I thought that it held a note of defiance. I guessed that he would rather have deferred breaking the good news until the coincidence of timing was less obvious.

It was the right moment to put the boot in – a process which I had never enjoyed during my banking days. 'I would expect you to be in a sound financial position,' I said. 'I hope you still will be after you've returned Mrs Ilwand's money to her.'

That stopped him in his tracks. I heard Bea Payne give a small gasp. Ian stiffened but remained silent. I thought that he was giving me rope and I was in some danger of hanging myself. Miles gaped at me but without real conviction. Like his late father, he was a poor actor. Bea was giving a much better portrayal of puzzlement and injured innocence. 'I don't know what you're talking about,' Miles said.

'Yes you do. The police have already tracked the money as far as Holland – where you've spent several days this week.'

'That doesn't prove anything. I have friends in the Netherlands.'

Ian, although he was still waiting in silence for me to produce some useful evidence, looked disapproving. I was breaking all the rules, warning the suspects before the time was ripe for charges to be brought. Miss McLure, however, was less inhibited by police protocol. 'We've got a bit further on since we last spoke to you,' she told me in her atrocious Glasgow accent. 'We know which bank the money was transferred to from Mrs Ilwand's account. By an arrangement arrived at over the phone, the money was withdrawn in cash. The transaction was so unusual that the staff remember it. When they were shown evidence of fraud, they furnished a description of the client.'

'The security video captured the customer,' Ian said reluctantly. 'It could well be yourself under the hat and the whiskers. No doubts the lawyers and their experts will argue interminably over just how good is the identification. The bank staff remember his British accent and would expect to identify him by his voice.'

'And we know the number of the mobile phone used to send the e-mails through the Agrotechnics mainframe and for the money transfers,' WDC McLure put in. 'It was purchased by, and registered to, Roger Breeks – in whose name the dummy bank accounts were opened.'

'You might try dialling the number,' I suggested, pushing the telephone across the desk towards her.

It was a long shot. The most likely outcome would have been nothingness. Or the call might have been answered by some scavenger who had found the phone on the local rubbish tip. Miles looked unconcerned and even slightly amused, but when I saw the perturbation that slipped through Bea Payne's careful mask I knew that it might hit the mark. The dialling was followed by a faint ringing in the other office. Otherwise there was a long silence. I heard footsteps outside the door. Miss McLure gently replaced the phone and the ringing next door stopped. Miles gave Bea a long look of reproach.

Bea Payne kicked Spin off her feet. The spaniel came to me for reassurance and lay down again. 'I deny everything,' Bea said through stiff lips. 'If there's a mobile phone in my office, it's been planted there.'

Miles closed his mouth with an audible snap. He tried to keep his face passive but I could see that his mind was racing.

'You should have had the sense to get rid of it,' I told Bea. 'Or at the very least to switch it off. Who were you expecting to call you on it?' I looked at Miles. 'It's all coming apart, isn't it? Why don't you make a clean breast of it and return Mrs Ilwand's money.'

'That really would be the best thing,' Ian said. He was watching Miss McLure's pencil. 'Of course, there's no compulsion on you to say anything, bearing in mind that this matter is certain to fetch up in court.'

'But must it?' Miles said. 'Suppose it was possible for me to make an admission and immediate restitution, would you advise Mrs Ilwand not to press charges?' he asked me.

'That,' Ian said slowly, 'is not a matter for Mrs Ilwand, it is a matter for the police. Of course, restitution and a clear statement, made prior to arrest, might count heavily in your favour. But it would have to be a full statement, mind. Juries tend to disbelieve arguments which are thought up later and weren't produced in the first statement.'

I hid a smile. There is no fixed wording for the statutory warning. Ian had managed to embed its meaning in a few apparently casual remarks.

Miles's carefully schooled mask failed him. Emotions chased themselves across his features. Guilt, fear, regret, they were all there. And anger. He turned on Bea Payne. 'I told you and told you to get rid of that thing,' he told her.

'I deny everything,' Bea said again. 'He's trying to shift the blame onto me.'

'I think Miss McLure should look in the computers,' I said. 'Both the desktop and the portable.'

198

Ian hesitated and then looked at Miles. 'Have you any objection?'

Miles was uneasy but he also looked puzzled. Was he, I wondered, so good an actor after all? Perhaps I had it all wrong. 'What if I have objections?' he asked.

'It will make almost no difference,' Ian said. 'We will have to proceed more slowly and officially, that's all. Meanwhile, somebody will stand guard over the machines.'

'In that case . . .' Miles said.

WDC McLure took this for permission. She switched on the laptop computer and left it to boot up. The desktop computer was almost in front of her, the screen readable. She pulled the keyboard round on its spiral cable. She touched no more than two or three keys. A new window appeared, overlaying part of the stock list on the screen.

Ian leaned towards it. 'What's that?'

'It's called the Recycle Bin,' said the WDC absently. 'Always the first place to look. It's where every file fetches up when it's been deleted.'

Miles looked at Bea. Her face remained stubborn and impassive.

'Most people,' the WDC continued, 'think that when you empty the Recycle Bin your deletions have gone for ever.'

'And they haven't?' I asked hopefully.

'No. All you've done is to remove them from the indexing system. They can still be found. It may take time or come easily . . .'

Bea showed momentary apprehension. For my part, I felt a glow of relief. Bea had treated her deletions as full and final.

Miles must have reached the same realization. 'Just

a minute,' he said quickly. 'I do have a strong objection. Anything in there has been deleted because it is totally and absolutely confidential. You have no right to pry into it.'

'As an investigating police officer,' Ian said, 'I have every right. In what way is the material confidential?'

'In every way.' He hesitated. 'The financial affairs of the business—'

'Agrotechnics will be taking over the business soon,' I said glibly. 'As a director, that gives me the right to see your figures.'

There was a huge hole in my argument, but it passed them by.

'But I've told you—' Miles began.

'Words are cheap,' I said. 'I haven't seen any cash yet.'

Miles turned back to Ian. 'Other things are confidential. All kinds. My father wrote his love letters on one or other of those machines.'

'What could have greater possible relevance to his death?' Ian asked.

During this argument, Miss McLure had been fingering the keys with her left hand, apparently idly, as if drumming her fingers on the desktop. But she had been tapping to good effect. The screen changed. 'One moment,' she said. She filled a page with her shorthand. 'Relevance to his death,' she repeated. She put down her pencil and returned her attention to the computer screen. 'Here we are,' she said. 'A copy of the fraudulent e-mail. The original, incoming one from Canada.'

'That doesn't mean a damn thing and you know it,' Miles said loudly. 'So somebody tried it on with us. Dad was going to give them their answers but I spotted it immediately for a try-on and that was an end to the matter.'

Ian looked at me but I had nothing to offer.

'Nothing else easy here that we'd consider significant,' said the WDC. 'It's going to take an hour or two to hunt out all the recent deletions.' She switched her attention to the laptop computer. Bea and Miles waited in sullen silence. 'Nothing here,' Miss McLure said suddenly. 'They'll have kept copies, if at all, on separate floppies. I'll have to gather them up and go through them all. Shall I go next door and make a start?'

Bea and Miles protested – loudly, as each tried to be heard above the other. Ian held up a hand as if to stop traffic. The gesture must have had some special significance or else his attitude held an authority which was lost on me, because they fell suddenly silent.

'You stay with us and keep a complete record,' Ian told the WDC. 'I want to hear what Mr Kitts has to say. Then, if I see fit, I'll impound every floppy in the place, including the house and the flat, and we'll take them away for you to study at your leisure.'

'Hypothetically,' Miles said desperately, 'just suppose that I was able to replace the money straight away and save all the delays and legal costs. What then?'

'Whether you get prosecuted or not depends on the police,' I said. 'And on whether you had a hand in your father's death.'

He turned white. 'For God's sake!' he yelped. 'I was out of the country. I wouldn't do such a thing. He was an old reprobate but he was my dad.'

'In that case,' I said, 'I'd be prepared to give you credit in court for your help and to state that I can appreciate

201

the pressure you felt under with your father frittering away your inheritance.'

'Now, just hold on a minute!' Ian broke in. 'You can't bargain with a suspect in the presence of the police.'

Having reached a winning position, I was not about to abandon it. 'I'm not bargaining,' I said. 'I'm stating the facts and expressing my views so that Mr Cowieson can reach a sensible decision. Agrotechnics would still call up the floating charge, take over the firm and put in a manager. If you escape a custodial sentence, I'll recommend that you are appointed on commission to carry out your rescue package. You will be audited every step of the way.'

Miles nodded slowly. 'And if . . . it goes the other way?'

'I'd be prepared to recommend that you're given the same terms when you come out.'

'But what about me?' Bea asked.

'I don't think that you will still be here,' I told her. 'I'm sorry.'

She began to change colour. I had seen her react to a daunting situation once before but this was in a new dimension altogether. Her face blanched chalky white but her cheeks, ears and chin flushed scarlet. The effect would have been comic except that her face, for one instant, showed terror before, with an effort that brought sweat to her throat and brow, it resumed its usual placid mien and the colours began to merge. 'I can't imagine what you mean,' she said. 'Unless you're giving me the sack.'

Ian had not missed the momentary revelation. I was playing fast and loose with the proper procedures but if I could show him where to look he could find the necessary evidence in proper form. He knew that I had already gone too far to withdraw. 'I think that you had better explain,' he said grimly.

What I wanted to say had been taking shape in my mind while the others argued. 'I'm in no doubt,' I began, 'that Miles Cowieson is Miss Payne's boyfriend and has been for some time.'

'No comment,' Miles said.

Bea nodded. 'That's nobody's damn business but ours,' she said.

'I suspect that Miles is the father of her unborn child – and you needn't bother to deny it,' I added when Miles opened his mouth to protest. 'A simple DNA test would confirm or refute that supposition. I'm sure that there's a relationship. Miss Payne reacted, minutely, whenever Mr Cowieson's name was mentioned.

'Let's call them Miles and Bea for the sake of brevity.

'I assume that Miles had been trying for some time to wear down his father's resistance, get her appointed to her present job and be given the granny flat. But the older man was addicted to false economies and no doubt objected to increasing the wages bill. I certainly can't see Mr Cowieson Senior, whose whole philosophy was summed up in the phrase Penny wise, pound foolish, taking on an office manager when he was stuck for cash and also quite convinced that he was the proverbial bee's knees at the job himself. However, Bea heard Mrs Ilwand say that she would want to ensure that existing employees were looked after and I later said much the same to Miles. That meant that Bea would be secure in the post provided that she was appointed before Agrotechnics called in the floating charge. They must have mounted an immediate assault and persisted until they had worn down the old man's resistance.' Another idea hit me and I blurted it out without thinking. 'Or they may have had a backup plan to kill old Maurice if he didn't come round.'

Miles and Bea began to protest. She fell silent and let him speak for her. 'This is preposterous,' he shouted. 'We don't have to stay here and listen to this.'

'No,' Ian said grimly. 'You don't. But I do and, if my superiors agree, you'll have to listen to it some time. I suggest that you hear Mr Kitts out now.' To me, he added, 'The times don't fit.'

That point had already struck me. 'You mean that Maurice was still alive while Bea was beginning her move into the granny-flat. But we only have her word for her movements.

'To go back to the beginning, putting together what you've told me with what I've found out for myself, Maurice Cowieson was running the firm rapidly towards bankruptcy or towards being taken over by the major creditor, Agrotechnics. Something had to be done or Miles would find himself without an inheritance, a job or prospects.' (Involuntarily, Miles nodded.) 'The first necessity was an injection of cash. The idea of an e-mail fraud was probably put into the heads of Bea and Miles when the first fraudulent e-mail came in. You may get your evidence of the outgoing copy from the floppies or from somewhere in one of the computers.'

Miss McLure nodded. 'It may take time, but I'll get it all out in the end.'

'I'm sure you will. So they disseminated their own version of the e-mail with a slightly different reply address, choosing recipients who they knew to be suitably wealthy and rather naïve and whose e-mail addresses they could obtain easily. Mrs Ilwand fits all three criteria and Bea had easy access to her papers and computers. You may find other examples among the attempted frauds lying with the Serious Fraud Office. The couple probably hoped that if two or three were foolish enough to reply they might at least win enough money to stave off the imminent takeover.

'Mrs Ilwand may not have been the only recipient daft enough to reply, but they must have been stunned to discover that they had gained access to her account at the one time when it held the proceeds of the farm sale, money intended for the share issue of Agrotechnics but more than enough to pay off Cowieson's debt to Agrotechnics. They would have to clean out the account, of course. To take only the amount due to Agrotechnics would have been an absolute giveaway.

'Whether Maurice Cowieson knew of this plot I rather doubt – he was a foolish, greedy and lecherous old goat and capable of monumental self-deception but I think he was fundamentally as honest as the next man – which probably means no more than being afraid of being caught out in dishonesty. I don't think that he would have gone along with a deliberate fraud. How they intended to explain the availability of the cash to him I can only guess. Possibly as a lottery win. Miles tried to hint to me that the money stemmed from organized crime. Perhaps he thought that that would seem credible and yet stifle enquiries. But that would never have washed with his father, who wouldn't have wanted his firm to get caught laundering money.'

I paused to gather my thoughts. My mouth was dry from too much talking. An incongruous water cooler was standing, American style, in the corner of the office and I got up to fill a paper cup. Not a word was spoken. Bea and Miles sat with the clear intention of hearing every word but avoiding any comment by word or deed. Ian seemed afraid to break the silence as long as anything potentially useful was emerging. Miss McLure passively completed her note-taking.

I wetted my mouth and resumed. 'Banks used to want references, postal addresses and your size in hats before they'd open an account but that's all changed. Nowadays, you can open an account over the phone with any name and password you care to choose and no questions asked. And the Dutch banks are more secretive even than the Swiss. So they had opened an account in Edinburgh to deal with incidental payments and a Dutch account to handle the big money. They could transfer the money from Mrs Ilwand's account into it, using Bea's laptop computer. They wouldn't want the telephone connection to be traced but they could have plugged the computer into a terminal almost anywhere – you see them at airports and railway stations and there are cafés that provide the facility. To make it even more difficult to follow their tracks they bought a digital mobile phone and routed their transaction through it and then through the mainframe at Agrotechnics.

'So far so good. But however secretive their moves had been, as we've just seen, traces are always left – records of telephone connections, computer transactions, electronic "footprints", bank records. If they set hands directly on the money, that too would be traced. Not easily, not quickly, but eventually. So it was necessary for Miles to go to Holland. The money was drawn out in cash. It may simply have been re-deposited in another bank or it may have been translated into something portable and very hard to trace. Possibly something documentary – what are loosely known as bearer bonds and cashier's cheques. But jewels and drugs are even more difficult to trace and Holland is ideal for either.

'Miles tells me that he expects to be in a position to settle accounts very shortly. Draw what inferences you like.

'Meanwhile, something happened back here. It may have been part of a prearranged plan or there may have been a sudden flare-up. Perhaps Maurice found out about the fraud and was going to expose it. His death may even have been unintended. Whatever the cause, Maurice died of a badly dented head. Quickly, he was loaded into his own car and driven to the road above the Den Burn. I believe that Bea was the driver and that she acted alone.'

Miles broke his silence at last. 'Bea, you didn't? You wouldn't!'

She shook her head, tight-lipped.

'Let's accept for the moment,' I said to Ian, 'that somebody behaved as I described. Much of what I've said came from you anyway. I've given you my interpretation but I leave it to you to make your own mind up. You discovered, as I did, that Mr Cowieson's car was driven by somebody unused to an automatic transmission. That person prepared to change down to make the turn at the top of the hill and made the common mistake of hitting the brake instead of the non-existent clutch. Bea is accustomed to driving around briskly in a car with manual gear-change and in the circumstances her mind may not have been wholly on her driving.'

'That doesn't prove anything,' Miles said desperately.

'It's another pointer,' I said. 'Arrived at her chosen place, where the little-used road turns sharply right away from a steep drop to the burn, she stopped and managed to move Maurice into the driving seat. Then, with the engine running and the lever in D for Drive, she let the handbrake off and walked beside the car, steering through the open window until it had picked up too much speed. It went over the brink. The car was probably intended to burn, covering up any possible traces of what had gone before. I don't know why it didn't.'

'It probably would have done,' Ian said, 'except that a rock smashed the sump and stopped the crankshaft, stalling the engine.'

'That would explain it. There was a stink of petrol. That, and the fact that Bea had been wearing her usual waxed cotton coat, prevented me from noticing the presence of her usual, rather strong, perfume in the car. I just don't understand why she didn't descend the embankment and drop a match.'

'If she had one,' Ian said.

'She always has matches,' I pointed out. 'She's a smoker. I've watched her. She snaps every match in half before discarding it.'

Ian said something under his breath which I failed to catch. 'Say that again?' I asked him.

He had been listening with a worried expression on his square face, but now he smiled. 'I thought so. Your hearing's deteriorated. I noticed that you're watching people's lips more than you used to.'

I dislike having my failing faculties discussed in public but I refused to take more than a small amount of umbrage. 'Even if that's true, is it relevant?'

'I think it is. You say the engine was still warm. How warm?'

'I already told you, I couldn't say. The exhaust was

still making clicking noises as it cooled, if that's any guide.'

'It is,' Ian said. 'I think that the car went down the embankment very shortly before you arrived there but you didn't hear it. Whoever sent the car down may have intended to climb down and set fire to it, but that would have taken time. Climbing down would have been very difficult at that place and traces would have been left. Before they reached the place where the beaters always climb down, they could see or hear you coming. So they abandoned that idea and hoped for the best. If you were still a couple of hundred yards off at the time and with the sound of the burn around you, would you have heard the crash?'

'Probably not,' I admitted. 'She – they, if you like – could have walked past me on the road before descending to the Den Burn and walking down the gully.'

'Or they could have walked the other way, met an accomplice and been driven home.'

'I think not. I think that the only possible accomplice was on his way to Holland.'

'There was no conspiracy,' Miles said angrily. 'You make any more suggestions like that and I'll sue you. And I can assure you that Bea never walked down the Den Burn.' He smiled ruefully. 'She hates country walking. I suggested once that she walk halfway down to meet me, and she thought that I'd gone mad. She said that she's left the country far behind her and as far as she's concerned it's for supplying the supermarkets and looking pretty on calendars.'

'Shut up, you fool,' Bea said furiously. 'Just listen.'

'Well, you did say that.' But Miles took another look at the strain on her face and fell suddenly silent again.

'I took the spaniel for a walk down the Den Burn this morning,' I said. 'He'd taken a fancy to Bea while she was staying in the house – look at him now.' Unnoticed, Spin had resumed his earlier position with his chin on her foot. 'Your men may have taken a look along the burn but they couldn't possibly have done a fingertip search and they didn't have a spaniel's nose. Spin picked this up and brought it to me.' I produced a small handkerchief from the polythene bag. 'It's very faint, but you can still smell her perfume on it. It has some very distinctive embroidery on it, the kind of thing that an aunt does for a favourite niece as a Christmas present. If Mrs Ilwand's staff did Bea's laundry they'll be able to identify it. They may even know if she had it with her on Sunday.'

'She could have walked down the Den Burn at any time,' Ian said.

'But she didn't. You just heard Miles. And Elizabeth says that Bea never developed the walking habit that most of us have in the country. She drives everywhere. It would take a very pressing need to get her out on foot. And then there were these.' I placed on the desk a broken match and the apple with tooth-marks.

Ian scowled at the exhibits. 'I sent three men down the Den Burn with orders to collect anything of even faintly possible significance. They wouldn't have missed the apple. So it was dropped later.'

'In point of fact,' I said, 'there was an apple tree nearby and if the apple was dropped among other wind-falls, and with the tooth-marks on the underside, who was going to notice? But, anyway, the apple had been placed on top of a section of wall. You couldn't see it from below. Some tidy-minded person had picked it up, started to bite into it, found that it was a cooking apple

210

and very bitter, and so placed it neatly out of the way on top of the wall because it was against their instincts to throw it down on the ground. Bea Payne is a compulsive tidier and she takes an apple every time she passes the bowl. Her teeth are very regular, as are the tooth-marks. I suggest that a forensic odontologist could easily prove the connection.'

As evidence, what I had brought out so far would have been of little use except perhaps for a question to be used in cross-examination. Ian was looking doubtful. But in Miles's eyes I could see shock and the dawning of reluctant belief. 'Bea,' he said, 'you didn't, did you?'

Bea Payne shot me a glance which, I swear, sent a chill through to my spine. It left me in no doubt that I was at the head of her list of People I would most like to eviscerate with a rusty razorblade. Then she looked at Miss McLure's still moving pencil. 'I deny it,' she said in a choked voice.

Miles seemed not to have heard her. 'My father?' he said wonderingly. 'You killed my father? Just because he found out about the e-mails and wouldn't go along?'

'No,' said Bea more loudly. What she was denying was unclear to me.

'He was my dad,' Miles said patiently, as though explaining something to himself. 'He was far from being a saint in some ways and he could be as thick as two planks in others, but he never stole. He shouldn't have died, it wasn't worth it, not for money. Bea, how could you do that to him? And to me?'

It was a measure of the hold that their relationship had on her mind that our presence seemed by now to be forgotten. Preserving his love for her outweighed any question of her own safety. When she spoke it was

211

directly to Miles, her eyes locked with his. She seemed to be pleading. 'It wasn't like that,' she said. 'I swear it wasn't. You'd told him that you were going to Holland to raise the wind on condition that you had a say in the running of the business and he seemed to accept that. He even said to me that he was getting too old for all the stress and that it would be a relief not to have to do all the worrying any more. But when I met him on Sunday he was suddenly a different man. You were away and that seemed to be what made the difference.

'I'd spent some time unpacking some of my things and arranging the flat the way I wanted it. I was happy at last. I had a job and you'd be nearby and we would be working together. And I loved my little flat. I'd never had space that was private to me before.

'The excitement of it kept me going until, all of a sudden, I realized that it was past lunchtime. I was hungry and I still had to get in some food. The supermarket stays open on a Sunday so I decided to drive down there and stock up.'

Ian, I noticed, had leaned forward very slowly and seemed to be looking out of the window. His bulk now screened WDC McLure and her darting pencil. Bea was not to be distracted, nor reminded that the law was listening.

'As I came down the outside stair your father came out of the front door. He waved cheerily and walked to meet me. He was very friendly and asked if I was settling in all right and I said that I was. As he came closer I could smell whisky on his breath. He was steady on his feet but he seemed somehow out of focus.

'He asked how long we'd known each other. I didn't want to anger him so I told him the truth, two years. But that wasn't enough, he grinned at me in a way I didn't like and asked me outright if we were sleeping together.'

Miles seemed more shocked than by any of her other disclosures. 'The old devil!' he said. 'What did you tell him?'

'It was none of his business. So I denied it. That was a mistake as it turned out. I was going to have to own up about the baby soon enough and meantime it left him feeling free to . . . to try his hand. He said that he was attracted to me and he began to make all sorts of suggestions.' She coloured. Tears were running freely but she ignored them. 'He didn't just want a roll in the hay. Some of what he said I won't ever repeat, even to you. I tried to laugh it off and I went to push past him but he looked round once to be sure that nobody was watching and then he grabbed me. There seemed to be hands everywhere, up my skirt, on my breasts and at the same time holding me so that I couldn't get away. He was trying to find my mouth and I could feel his stubble and his tongue and the smell of drink was strong and I wanted to be sick. I would have bitten him except that I couldn't have borne having any part of him in my mouth.'

She drew a shuddering breath and went on. 'I had one arm free and in a sort of desperation I punched him low down as hard as I could and then gave him a push. He let go then and I fell, almost into the trench. He was doubled up above me but, looking up, it seemed as though he'd be ten feet tall if he straightened and he was furious, hurt physically as well as in his pride. His face had gone scarlet. And he was saying awful things. That I was sacked was the least of them. You wouldn't believe what he was going to do to me. He bent down further and grabbed me by the elbow. "Into the house," he said.

213

'The way I'd fallen, my hand closed on a piece of
pipe and before I could think what to do I'd hit him with
it. I didn't want to kill him but I didn't want to be dragged
inside and have the things he'd been talking about done
to me.' She drew breath in a shuddering sigh. 'I didn't
mean to hit him so hard, but I was in a panic. He fell
down. I couldn't find a pulse and he wasn't breathing and
there was a squashy dent in his head and where the skin
was broken it only bled for a second or two and then
stopped. I was horrified. I threw the piece of pipe into
the bottom of the trench and knelt down. I forced myself
to try the kiss of life but he never breathed on his own
and even the tiniest twitchings stopped. I knew, I absolutely knew, that he was dead. After that, it was just as
Mr Kitts told it. Miles, do you forgive me?' she asked
urgently.

There was silence, as if sound had been switched off.
I think that we were all as curious to know the answer
to her question as we had been to hear the rest of her
story. Spin sat up and pawed her leg, offering comfort,
but he was ignored.

Miles took a large handkerchief from his breast pocket
and handed it to her. She began to dry her face which
was soaked with tears. 'I think so,' he said at last. 'You'll
have to give me time.'

Bea breathed again. She blew her nose and wiped her
eyes. 'You believe me, then?'

'Oh yes. I believe you. There had been one or two
other incidents, when he'd been drinking. I've managed
to smooth them over until now. He . . . he always
accepted that he'd been wrong and tried to make it all
right with gifts and an apology.' He sighed. 'I believe you
all right.'

'And you'll stand by me if I go to jail? And look after my baby?'

'If I can. For as long as it takes. It's my baby too.'

Bea sighed deeply and then her old, peevish expression made a return. 'That damned mobile phone!' she said. 'If it weren't for that, there'd have been no proof. I was going to throw it away and get a replacement, but I had to go out for an hour this morning so I left its number with the girls, to call me if anything came up, and took it with me. And then I forgot all about it.'

Later, when the formalities had been observed and I met Ian to get my statement down on paper, I reminded him of Miles's words.

'For as long as it takes,' I echoed. 'That's what he said. How long do you think that will be?'

'Who can tell how a judge and jury will react? But my guess is that if she pleads guilty, sheds a few more tears, tells that story as convincingly as she did to us and sticks to it, that may not be for very long. The courts tend to be sympathetic to a woman defending her honour. And undoubtedly the defence can produce witnesses to Maurice Cowieson's bad behaviour in the past. We've heard tales.'

'And him?' I asked.

Ian shrugged. 'A first offender, promising good behaviour and with a job to go to? Not very much. He might even get off with a fine and community service.'

There was something missing. It took me a few seconds to think what it was. 'You've only discussed whether a judge and jury would believe her. But do *you* believe her?' I asked him. 'Or was it really over the money?'

'That's quite a different matter.' He looked at me speculatively, holding my eye. 'You're inviting me to guess what was in a woman's mind on a particular occasion, several days ago. What do you yourself think?'

'She's a competent actress – I never detected anything odd in her manner when I met her the next day, or no more than could have been explained by finding herself suddenly in sole charge of the business. Was there whisky in his stomach?'

Ian tapped the post mortem report on his desk. 'No doubt of it. He was carrying about twice the limit set for the breathalyser. That was the one thing that lent credibility to the accident theory. And I'll tell you another thing. Professor Manatoy – remember him? – he did the autopsy himself and he's very thorough. He says that the corpse showed distinct signs of recent sexual excitement.'

'And, of course, you have to hand that over to the defence,' I said. 'So who cares what the truth is? If she puts over her story as dramatically as she did, she'll get off with about three years for manslaughter and serve maybe two.'

'As much as that?' Ian said. 'With a baby to carry into court? I doubt it. And she'll sell her story to the tabloids for enough to buy the firm back from you. Who says that crime doesn't pay?'

'Nobody, these days,' I said. 'And how about yourself. How have you come out of it? Not too many ructions within the Force?'

He grinned suddenly and I realized that he had with difficulty been containing some secret joy. 'I let you do your thing,' he said, 'when I should really have shut you up and carted you back here. But I decided that it was a heads I win, tails you lose situation. If you blew it, you'd carry all the blame and probably get sued for slander. But it worked. When I produced the two accused, they were still preoccupied with purging their souls and confessing like mad to anybody who would listen.

'Mr Dornoch had sent in a damning report about me. And he'd just arrested and charged the builder, Allardyce.'

NEATH PORT TALBOT LIBRARY							
AND INFORMATION SERVICES							
1		25		49		73	
2		26		50		74	
3		27		51		75	
4		28		52		76	
5		29		53		77	
6		30		54		78	
7	4|19	31		55		79	
8		32		56		80	
9		33		57		81	
10		34		58		82	
11		35		59		83	
12		36		60		84	
13		37		61		85	
14		38		62		86	
15		39		63		87	
16		40		64		88	
17		41		65		89	
18		42		66		90	
19		43		67		91	
20		44		68		92	
21		45		69		COMMUNITY SERVICES	
22		46		70			
23		47		71		NPT/111	
24		48		72